WRENCHED

CASEY MORALES

DEDICATION

To all the men and women who serve, and to those who support them. You are loved and appreciated. Thank you.

CHAPTER ONE

MIGUEL: THE CALL (FRIDAY, JUNE 5, 9:50 A.M.)

Donna and I didn't normally sit around the station with nothing to do. But for some reason, this morning had been pleasantly free of murder or other violent crimes. That made the coffee taste just a little better.

Then Sergeant Brandt barked from his office doorway: "Nuñez, Frazier, my office, now."

Donna rose and looked back. "Come on, Smiley. Don't want to keep the Grinch waiting."

"Shit," I said, tossing down the last of my coffee and pushing back from my desk.

Brandt was fiddling with his keyboard when we entered and didn't look up. "Close the door and sit."

He was never one to mince words.

As we sat, the recording of a phone call crackled through his speakers. A mechanical voice said, "Emergency operator call, Tuesday, June 5, 8:33 a.m."

"*Nine-one-one, what is your emergency?*" a female voice asked.

A deep baritone trembled with each word. "*My wife didn't come home last night or this morning. She hasn't called either.*"

"*Your wife is missing?*"

"*Yes. That's what I just said,*" the man snapped.

"*Please stay calm, sir. When did you see her last?*"

There was a brief pause. "*Ten—no, eleven o'clock yesterday morning.*"

"*Sir, we generally don't record a person as missing before twenty-four hours have passed unless they are a minor, there is a break-in, or some other sign of foul play. Do you have any reason to believe your wife was the victim of a crime?*"

Another pause. "*No. But she's never disappeared like this without calling. This isn't like her.*"

"I understand your concern, but why don't we wait a few more hours and see if she turns up. That's what happens ninety-nine percent of the time."

"And what about the other one percent? What if the hours we wait put her life at risk?" His voice was rising. *"I don't want to wait."*

"Sir, I've made notes of your call, but until we've passed the twenty-four hours, or until you can provide some evidence of foul play, there's nothing our investigators can do." When the man didn't respond, the operator said, *"I get that you're scared. Try to stay calm. Call her friends, anyone she might've stayed with last night. You can start asking around before we get involved."*

"So, you want me to do your *job? Is that it?"* The man's voice was white-hot now. *"Fuckin' waste of time."*

Click.

"That was three days ago, which means she's been missing four. Husband went to Channel 4, so there's heat on this now. The mayor's pissed we didn't jump on it sooner and tore the chief a new one early this morning. Never mind how many crank calls we get like this every day. You're as downhill as the shit can roll, so congrats for catching it." Brandt pushed his keyboard away, then shoved a thin file toward us.

"House search?" Donna asked.

"Husband consented over the phone. Ball's in your court, just get the paperwork signed and coordinate with CSI."

"CSI?" I couldn't hide my surprise. "You already think this is more than—"

Brandt raised his palm. "I'm not saying anything, just that you need to get everybody in the boat, alright?"

I sat back as an uneasy itch crawled up my neck.

"I've already looped in the deputy chief in case we need detectives assigned. The morning brief put the wife's face in front of every cop in the city. That should help. Come back to me with what you need, but find this one fast, alright?"

"Yes, Sarge," we said in unison.

Brandt turned away from us and began pecking at his keyboard with the only two fingers he knew how to use. I resisted the easy joke, though it took an effort. Donna snatched the file and we strode back to our desks.

"He's all warm and fuzzy this morning," I quipped.

Donna sat at her desk and opened the file without looking up or responding.

"No one's been to visit the husband yet." She read a moment. "Huh. He hasn't been here either. That's odd."

I raised a brow. "Odd? A man whose wife is missing and probably feels like the police aren't doing shit doesn't want to visit the station? Sounds about right to me."

"Yeah, all that." She shrugged. "Still seems a little weird. I'd yell at anyone who'd listen if my husband went missing."

"He yelled into the cameras, probably just to get us to listen—and it worked."

"True." She nodded then closed the file. "There's nothing in here. Husband's a writer and works out of his house. Let's go see him."

CHAPTER TWO

MIGUEL: FIRST CONTACT (FRIDAY, JUNE 5, 11 A.M.)

We pulled into the driveway of a sprawling, ranch-style brick home in the heart of Green Hills. The shrubbery was neatly trimmed, and rows of colorful flowers bloomed in boxes hung from each window. The front door opened before Donna turned off the engine and the silhouette of a man appeared in the entranceway.

Donna took the lead. She usually did. She asked questions while I sat back and observed. A lot of guys on the force couldn't shove their ego down long enough to let that happen, but it worked for us.

I'd been with the force for a couple years longer, but she was better at putting people at ease. I learned a lot watching her work. She was born for this. She had a sharp mind and an even keener eye. It wasn't always easy having a partner, but Donna kept things light, as much as was possible when dealing with death all day. Over the years, she'd become more like an older sister than the rookie cop I was assigned to train. Hell, it felt like she was training *me* most of the time.

"Mr. Shale?" Donna said when we reached the two steps that led to the front door.

The man opened the screen door and stepped out. "Yes. I'm Karl. Come in, please."

Donna extended a hand with both our business cards, and he took them. As we entered, she said, "I'm Officer Frazier. This is Officer Nuñez."

"About time you guys showed up." Karl led us into a sitting area just inside the entrance and motioned to the couch opposite a large overstuffed chair, where he sat. "Can I get you anything? Coffee?"

"No, we're fine." Donna waved him off. "We understand you reported your wife missing a few days ago—"

"Three days ago. And I had to go on TV just to get you here." He looked away from us.

Donna didn't flinch. "We're here to help, Mr. Shale. What can you tell us about the morning you last saw your wife? That was the first?"

"Yeah, Monday." He nodded and returned his gaze to Donna. "She left around eleven in the morning to run errands."

"What kind of errands?"

"I don't know. The usual kind. She said she was going to the grocery store, but she'd normally hit other places while she was out. She did that most Mondays, planning meals for the week and such. I didn't think anything about it."

"Which stores did she usually shop at?"

He rattled off the nearby Kroger, CVS, and a few others.

"Did you see her leave?"

"Sure. Kissed her goodbye."

"And her car?"

He cocked his head. "What about her car?"

"Did you see her drive away?"

"Well, uh, no." He thought a moment, then leaned forward. "I heard the garage door open, but walked back to my office and didn't hear anything else. Why would you—"

Donna held up a palm. "I'm just trying to get a feel for the timeline."

He nodded and sat back.

"She hasn't called or texted since that morning?" Donna asked.

"No."

"Have you talked with any of her friends or relatives, people she speaks with regularly?"

"Of course I have," he snapped. "Her sister, two of her best friends, people at her work."

"Can you write down the names and numbers of the people you contacted? Also, the names and numbers of any others you think she might contact?"

"Yeah. All that's in my computer in my office." He made to stand.

"Great. We'll follow you."

The trek down the hallway gave us a cursory glance into several rooms. The walls of Karl's office were overstuffed with books. Shelves upon shelves were so filled the wood was bowing under the weight. His desk was a wreck too, with printouts and open books piled atop one another.

Sticky notes covered most of one wall. A few had apparently fallen off enough times that he'd resorted to push pins to keep them up.

"A sticky-note wall?" I asked, scanning the scribbles on the yellow squares.

"It's how I plot my stories. It's easy to move chapters around that way."

"Huh. What kind of books do you write?" Donna asked.

"Mostly mysteries, though some cross over into thriller territory. The line between the two can be kind of gray."

Karl sat behind his desk and pecked at the keys rapidly, then tore off a sheet from a pad and began writing. By the time he handed the paper to Donna, there were twelve names and phone numbers listed.

Donna scanned it, then glanced up. "Her parents? They're not listed. Are they still alive?"

"Yeah, they're both alive." He blew out a sigh. "I didn't want to worry them yet." Several heartbeats passed before Karl spoke again. "Look, they hate me, always have, since before we got married. I'm not trying to keep anything from them, but they'd just find a way to get pissed at me rather than help."

Donna made a note. "I'd like their names and numbers anyway, please."

He leaned forward and punched a few keys, then read the information aloud for Donna to jot down.

"Do you remember anything else about that morning? Maybe something that seemed innocent then, but now feels odd?"

"No, it was a normal Monday morning." He looked up at the ceiling, then back to Donna. "I'm about five thousand words into the first book of my new series, and the first ones always suck the life out of me. You have to create everything from scratch: the characters, the setting, the story, sometimes the whole world. I was absorbed; I wasn't really paying much attention to anything else."

"What does Mrs. Shale do for work? You mentioned talking with some of her coworkers."

"She works part-time for the United Way heading up some of their fundraising drives."

"That's impressive. Has she always worked for nonprofits?" I asked.

"No. She spent a dozen years working in finance for a big bank. That's where she got all the connections to help the charities."

I nodded. "Makes sense."

"Does your wife drink?" Donna asked.

Karl's face darkened. "What does that have to do with anything?"

"Please, Mr. Shale."

"Yeah, she likes wine now and then, but she's not some drunk, if that's what you're asking."

"I'm just ruling things out." She clicked her pen and slid it into the spiral of her notepad, but didn't close the cover. "Mind if we look around a bit?"

"No, of course not." Karl stood. "Bedrooms are back there. Kitchen is down that hallway."

"And the garage?"

"It's through the kitchen, door by the fridge."

"Would you mind giving us a tour?" Donna asked. I knew she was just keeping him in our sights as we searched the place. If he didn't come with us, procedure would've required I stay to babysit him while she poked around.

"Yeah, sure. Whatever you need."

Afterward, as we walked back into the living room, I handed Karl a consent form, allowing us to return and conduct a more thorough search.

"You think this is necessary? To search our house? Didn't you just do that?" he asked before I could explain.

"We appreciate the walk-through. It gave us a feel for the place, but wasn't a thorough search. If there's even the smallest chance we could find something to help us locate your wife, it's worth it. Think of it as turning over every stone."

He stared a heartbeat, then grabbed a pen off a side table and signed.

⸻◦⸻

"Thoughts?" Donna asked as we pulled out of the Shales' driveway. She used the same one-word question after every interview. I chuckled at her consistency.

"Not a lot to go on. Husband seems genuinely worried, and I don't get the abuser vibe from him. No alarm bells there."

"Yeah. Agreed. Bottles in the liquor cabinet were dusty, and I only saw one wine bottle in the rack. I don't think we have a drunk on a binge here." She pulled onto the main road. "That was some garage though."

The Shales' garage was a home mechanic's wild dream. Tall metal cabinets lined one wall, while a tool-laden pegboard covered the side with the kitchen door. Unlike Karl's office, the garage was immaculate, with every tool clean and perfectly in place.

"Guess so. A lot of guys like their tools."

Donna rolled her eyes at me. She did that a lot, but I knew the smile beneath them meant she was more amused than anything.

"I'm resisting the easy joke, gay boy, but it's hard."

I snorted. "You said hard."

That earned another, much more dramatic eye roll.

"Seriously though, I've seen repair shops with fewer tools," she said. "He had everything but a lift in there. Floor even had that blue paint like you see in showrooms, though he had let oil pool in a few places. One spot looked fresh."

"You really don't miss much, do you?"

"Not if I want to make detective one day."

I never doubted she'd trade in her uniform for a suit one day, not for a minute. She was the sharpest cop I'd ever worked with, and would be the best detective Nashville had ever seen.

"So, what now?" I asked.

Donna's eyes shifted as she ticked through a mental checklist. "It's already three thirty. Let's hit the station and start calling through this list. Since the husband looks clean, we can do the house search tomorrow. Let's have some other uniforms canvas the neighbors and stores he mentioned, and I'll have her credit cards and bank accounts flagged. Oh, can you coordinate the house search?"

"Sure, sounds good."

CHAPTER THREE

MIGUEL: ALL HANDS (SATURDAY, JUNE 6, NOON)

I didn't usually relax and do nothing. My mind wouldn't let me, and the idea of sitting around made my muscles twitch. But I'd woken with a headache and wanted nothing more than to drink coffee, eat some grocery store croissants, and watch whatever game ESPN had decided to air. It didn't matter who played. It was baseball, and that demanded I watch it.

I made it a few minutes into *SportsCenter*. They'd just teased the game that would start at one p.m. when my phone buzzed.

Donna: Smiley, Sarge wants us in the station. Financials are back.

I let my head fall back on the couch cushion and debated pretending I'd never seen the text. Donna would kill me. It wasn't worth it. I tossed back the last of my now-cold coffee and punched on the screen.

Me: Gotta shower. Be there in thirty.

Donna was poring over a stack of papers when I arrived. I set a Starbucks cup on her desk, then another on mine. She grabbed the cup, took a sip, then grunted, all without looking up.

"Other than recurring charges, there hasn't been a single transaction on any of Emily Shale's accounts this month. Not one."

"That takes us back to the day the husband reported her missing? June first?" I asked.

She nodded. "Yeah."

She leaned forward and squinted at the screen, while I stared at the ceiling fan.

"That's pretty weird, isn't it?" I said absently.

"Weird?" Donna gave me the 'you aren't a dumb rookie' look. "If we assume she was kidnapped, it's actually pretty normal."

"Right. I get that, but hang with me," I said. "The husband said she left to run errands, right? She was going *shopping*."

"Well, shit." Recognition dawned on Donna's face.

"Shouldn't there be something on the first? I mean, unless she was kidnapped between her house and the grocery store, or wherever she went first, wouldn't there be at least one charge? She could've paid cash, I guess, but who does that at the grocery store when buying for a whole week?"

Donna's gaze fixed on mine.

"I was hoping this was gonna be routine, that she'd run off with a lover or just left a lousy husband. Shit. This looks bad."

I started to agree, but was startled by Sergeant Brandt's sudden appearance at our desks. "Dispatch just got a call from a hiker who found a car matching Emily Shale's."

"Where?" I asked.

"Edwin Warner Park," he said. "By the time you get there, our guys should have the area roped off."

Without another word, Donna and I raced toward the door.

———◆———

Edwin Warner Park was one of the largest and most scenic nature reserves in the area, only nine miles from the heart of downtown Nashville. Its thirty-one hundred acres included historic sites such as a World War I memorial dedicated to the First Tennessee Infantry, stacked-stone walls that have stood for more than two hundred years, the Iroquois Steeplechase Grounds, wide open fields, and lush, forested grounds. Paved walking paths and dirt hiking trails crisscrossed the landscape, and, while much of the park remained open to the public, there were large old-growth sections restricted to park rangers and wildlife professionals.

Emily Shale's blue Honda was parked on a remote, heavily forested corner of the park where even the rangers rarely set foot. Deep ridges scored the grass where it had driven through a hundred yards of soggy ground. Police cruisers were parked haphazardly beside a green ranger pickup in the nearest lot a football field's length away.

A wide perimeter had been established around the car and was cordoned off by yellow and black crime scene tape. Several uniformed officers milled about, looking more interested in keeping mud off their shoes than searching for evidence. Two rangers leaned against a tree watching the scene unfold.

As we slogged our way across the bog-like field, Donna pointed off to the right, where another uniformed officer was chatting with a twenty-something guy in dark shorts, a blue cap, and a white Predators T-shirt.

"You guys bring coffee? Sarge said you were taking care of us," one of the cops guarding the scene called as we approached.

"Uber Eats was right behind us. Were you the jackass who ordered the steak?" Donna never missed a beat. When the guys' laughter settled, she asked, "Who was first on scene?"

"He was." Coffee Cop pointed toward the officer with the civilian.

Donna nodded her thanks as we headed in that direction. She was about to introduce herself when a golden retriever bounded into view from the forest and planted muddy prints on the witness's shirt.

"Hey, buddy. Down. Get down," the man said, as he struggled to get the excited dog off his chest. "Sorry, Officer, Pekka's just bored."

"Pekka?" I asked. "Like the goalie?"

"Yeah. You a Preds fan?"

I nodded. "You bet. Best team in Smashville."

I surprised the guy by poking my fist out, and he gave me a bump.

Seeing the quick connection, Donna stepped back and let me handle the conversation.

"Nuñez and Frazier," I said by way of introduction to the cop, sticking a hand out for him to shake.

"Miller. He's all yours. I've got your scene secured. Let me know if you need anything." He turned to the muddy civilian as he started to walk away. "Thanks for your help. You're in good hands here."

The witness's name was Mike Alcott. He walked his dog in the park almost every day, usually in the early morning. He said he was late getting to the park today, and Pekka was restless and darted away as soon as he was freed from his leash.

"Took me nearly thirty minutes to get him to stop running away from me. I've never been back in this part of the park, and kind of got lost. That's when I looked up and saw that car."

"What time was this?"

"Maybe an hour ago. What's that? Ten thirty? Eleven o'clock?"

I nodded and made a note.

"Did you see anyone while you were out here looking for Pekka?"

"No. It would've been really peaceful if I hadn't been chasing my beast."

"What about when you got to the car? Was there anyone here?"

"No. It was totally abandoned."

"Did you look inside? Open it up?"

Mike shook his head. "I knew better than to do that. They were talking about a blue Honda on the news this morning."

"What made you think this might be that car? I mean, other than that it's a blue Honda?"

"The personalized plate kinda jumped out."

I peered over his shoulder to the car. The plate read, UNTDWAY.

"Yeah, that's one of a kind." I skimmed my notepad, then asked, "Did you happen to lean up against the car? Touch it at all?"

He nodded. "Before I saw the plate, I felt the hood to see if it'd been running."

"And?"

"Stone cold."

I made another note.

"Alright, Mike. Anything else you can think of?"

"No. I called you guys from my cell right away. That park ranger came out almost immediately. Police cars started showing up maybe ten minutes later."

"I'm sure Officer Miller got your contact info, but mind giving it to me again, just so we have it handy?" He rattled off his full name, address, and phone number. Then I dug out a business card and handed it to him. "If you think of anything else, call us. We really appreciate your help."

"You bet." He started to turn, then looked up. "You think she's still alive? The news said she's been missing several days, now her car turns up in a park?"

"We hope so, Mike. We really do."

He nodded, realizing that was all the information he would get. He called for Pekka and the golden dutifully bounded up to be leashed. He was a dozen paces away when he called back over his shoulder. "Hey, Officer Nuñez."

"Yeah?"

"Go Preds!"

I gave him a thumbs-up and a smile. When I turned back toward the car, Donna was shaking her head and chuckling.

"What? Can't a guy be nice? He's a hockey fan, after all."

"I swear you would hit on a tree if you thought it had a—"

"Hey! I was just being polite and professional, like they taught us at the academy."

"Uh-huh. Bring your polite and professional ass over here and let's check out this car."

"Yes, Mom ... I mean, ma'am."

She shook her head again as we dug out our rubber gloves and made our way to the car.

The windows were rolled up, but the doors were unlocked. The tires sat in deep ruts where the car's weight had sunk it further into the mud. I walked around, looking for damage or some sign of an accident, but didn't find anything worse than splattered mud.

A few footprints, likely made by a man's shoes, headed away from the passenger's door. The mud held their shape fairly well, but details were obscured by a thick layer of overgrown grass that was pressed into them. I doubted we'd be able to pick any sole patterns.

Donna opened the driver's-side door and stuck her head inside. A moment later, she clicked her flashlight on and scanned the floorboards.

"There's blood in the back seat, passenger's side. A lot of it. The rest of the car looks empty. Doesn't look like it's been wiped down."

We walked the perimeter, then expanded our search further out. There were a few indentations near the car where someone had walked from the driver's side around the front to the back seat passenger's side, then away from the vehicle. The ground rose slightly and firmed as we left the immediate area where the car sat, and the prints vanished only a few feet away. I leaned down and scanned the ground near the passenger's side, then pulled out my phone and zoomed in to get a closer look.

"Anything?" Donna asked from a few feet away.

"Yeah, looks like some blood streaks headed in that direction." I followed the streaks with my hand and pointed into the nearby woods, then rose and stepped back to avoid contaminating the scene further. Without a word, Donna and I followed the blood smears, each of us walking a good ten paces to either side. When we got to the edge of a dense stand of trees, Donna stopped.

"We'd better call all this in and let detectives take over," she said.

"Any chance she's alive and needs medical?"

Donna gave me her 'you aren't being serious, are you?' look.

I grabbed my cell and punched in Sergeant Brandt's number. A terse two-minute conversation later, I shoved the phone back in my pocket.

"He's on it. Hard lid on media. I'll go tell the guys and put a muzzle on the ranger."

She nodded absently. "Have them expand the tape. This part of that park is closed to the public, but we need to make sure the rangers keep out of this area too."

"Or another Pekka," I quipped.She didn't smile.

Donna and I circled the car one last time, then headed back across the field toward our cruiser.

"Looks like it's time to call in the big guns," I said, earning a sharp glare from the officers. "Easy with those lasers. I just meant this is now a likely homicide."

———◦———

An hour later, Donna and I were halfway through lunch at Soy Cubano, a small restaurant on the northeast side, when her phone buzzed.

"Frazier," she answered.

After a moment's pause, I heard, "Shit. Okay. Thanks for the call. We should be back at the station in twenty or thirty minutes."

The caller spoke again, then she disconnected and leaned back in her chair.

I raised a questioning brow.

"They found Emily."

"Okay. Where?"

"In those woods. The back of her head was bashed in."

CHAPTER FOUR

SAM: ALL IN A DAY'S WORK (SATURDAY, JUNE 6, 5:10 P.M.)

I tossed the clipboard onto the desk and rubbed my burning eyes. Saturdays at the shop sucked. I didn't have a life, so I worked most Saturdays, but they fell into one of two categories: insanely busy or mind-numbingly boring.

Between an endless stream of paperwork and an eternal morning meeting with my accountant, the day had been a bust. I loved plunging my hands deep into the belly of an ailing mechanical beast, but digging into spreadsheets and contracts made my temples ache.

I glanced up at the clock and debated slipping out a little early to hit the gym. The shop didn't close until seven, but I wasn't getting any work done, and a good workout always cleared the cobwebs and put me in a better mood.

Then the shop bell rang. A car had driven onto the lot.

A strange squealing noise was followed by a series of loud clanks. Curiosity won over boredom, and I stood to peek out my office window. A firetruck-red 1955 Chevy Bel-Air, one of the most sought-after collector cars on the market, rolled to the edge of the garage bays. The car was clearly sick, but she was a beauty. There wasn't a single dent or scratch on her brilliant cherry and white paint, and her silver chrome gleamed. Even the walls of the tires were spotless as newly cleaned teeth. Only the convertible top showed any sign of age or wear in the form of wrinkles in the fabric where metal had pressed against it for years.

My heart skipped a beat as I stepped out of my office. Two of my guys stopped their work and whistled in appreciation.

I made my way to the driver's door and helped an elderly woman climb out from behind the wheel.

"Hi there. I'm Sam." I felt suddenly awkward. My name was scrawled in cursive across a patch sewn onto my bowling-style shirt. "Sure is a beautiful car you have there. What can we do for you, ma'am?"

"I'm Marjorie, Marjorie Polk. Nice to meet you, Sam." The woman's weathered hand gripped mine with surprising strength. "Do you work on old Chevrolets?"

I smiled. "Yes, ma'am. We work on pretty much anything with an engine and wheels."

"That's what I heard," she said.

Mrs. Polk explained the car jerked when changing gears, and made strange noises. She tried to replicate the noises with her tongue and lips, but ended up sounding more like someone's flatulence than her majestic machine. We both laughed at her effort.

I liked the woman immediately.

"Well, ma'am, from what I heard when you pulled in, it could be a few different things. I really won't know until I test her out, then get a look under the hood."

"Honey—I mean, Sam—you do whatever you need to. When you figure it out, call me, okay? This car means the world to me."

I cocked my head curiously.

"My husband, bless his soul, loved this car more than anything. He tinkered with it for nearly forty years without ever really driving it. I never saw the point, but it made him happy." She smiled, and her eyes became distant. "I lost him last year ..."

I waited as the woman sucked in a wobbly breath.

"Anyway, I'd do anything to keep this thing alive. Please, Sam, can you help me?"

My heart clenched as she gazed at me with watery eyes.

"I'll do my best." I looked back at the car as a thought occurred to me. "If it's the transmission, this could get expensive. Finding parts for a car this old—"

"Sam." Her firm voice startled me almost as much as her sudden grip on my arm. "I'm old and I'm rich. I don't care what it costs. A good friend sent me here, said you're as honest as they come. You be fair, and I'll be grateful, alright?"

"Yes, ma'am. I can promise you that.""Good. Now, I'll leave you to it." She turned, then a schoolgirl giggle escaped.

"Mrs. Polk?" I asked.

She turned back with a sheepish grin. "I completely forgot. I don't have a car to drive home."

I couldn't help but smile. The woman's infectious warmth was exactly what I'd needed after the day I'd had.

"I'm happy to get you an Uber."

"Oh, I don't want to be a bother. I just live up the street."

"It's no bother. Come in and relax while I call you a car."

A heartbeat later, I watched as Mrs. Polk folded her elderly frame into a black sedan. She turned back and waved.

I grinned and mirrored the gesture, then strode over to the ailing Chevy and pulled her into the bay. I would normally assign new customers to one of my guys, but not this one. I couldn't resist the idea of working on such a classic car.

Nearly three hours later, parts lay strewn across a blue paper tarp, and I was no closer to finding the issue.

Frustrated, I shuffled into the restroom to clean the afternoon off my skin.

"Why am I so exhausted when I didn't really do anything useful?" I muttered as I pumped another two squirts of soap onto my hands. I might not have been able to fix anything, but I would get the darn grease out from under my nails.

"Hey, boss." The familiar voice of Tyler Hyatt broke through my brooding. Tyler was my first employee when I opened the shop, and we'd grown into something more like brothers than coworkers over the years.

"Yeah?"

"Looks like a tow's bringing something in. You expecting anything this late?" Tyler asked.

"What? No. Nobody called anything in." I glanced up to see it was nearly seven o'clock. "Just tell 'em to drop it in the lot. We can deal with it in the morning."

"Aye, aye, cap'n." Sam grinned at Tyler's mock salute.

A moment later, I was still scrubbing when Tyler's head popped into the doorway.

"Uh, Sam, you'll want to get out here."

My eyes snapped to Tyler's through the mirror.

"There are cops here."

<hr />

I was still drying my hands on a dingy towel as I ventured out. A blue Honda Accord was chained atop a tow truck's bed. From what I could see, there didn't appear to be any damage.

A van whose markings read Crime Scene Investigation Unit pulled into the lot behind the tow truck. More flashing blue lights drew my attention as a cruiser turned in and parked behind the van.

I watched as two officers emerged from the cruiser and headed toward me. A hulking man who looked like his body was trying to escape his uniform trailed behind a tiny woman.

"Are you Sam Prescott?" the woman asked when they were a few feet away. The male cop hid behind reflective glasses, with one hand on his hip and the other resting on the handle of his gun like he might shoot me at any minute.

That was reassuring.

"Yes, ma'am. What's all this?" I waved a hand toward the tow truck and crime van.

"I'm Officer Frazier. This is my partner, Officer Nuñez." Frazier handed me a business card. "Have you heard the name Emily Shale?"

I nodded. "The missing woman? Sure. It's all over the news."

"That's her car." She hooked a thumb toward the Honda. "A hiker found it a few hours ago."

"Okay." I glanced up at Nuñez. He hadn't moved, not even a twitch. A dark shadow covered his angular jaw.

I looked back at Frazier. "What's it doing here? I've worked with the department before, mostly fixing cruisers when your shop is slammed. This seems like something you'd want to keep in-house. And I've never had a surprise visit. They always call ahead of time. You guys love your paperwork more than any customer I've met."

"Yeah, tell me about it." Frazier snorted, the first hint there was a human beneath her mask. I caught a quirk at the corner of Nuñez's mouth too. "Tow company screwed up. They were supposed to take it to a shop in Brentwood. That's where the CSI boys usually work when our garage is full. They've got video surveillance and individual bays that lock so we can secure vehicles without worrying about contamination. I'm not sure how your place got printed on the order by mistake."

"Weird."

"Yeah." Frazier pulled a small notebook from her chest pocket and flipped a few pages. "According to my supervisor, you've been on the department's authorized list for a while, so they gave me an approval code to switch to your garage. Have room for one more?"

I shrugged. "Sure, I guess. But I'm still confused as to why you need a repair shop. What do you want me to do with it?"

"If you could let the department rent a bay for a few days, our guys will do their work, then we'll tow the car away when space opens up back at our garage. CSI guys need to do their thing. We'll need to close off one of your bays, then tape and lock it."

"That's easy enough. There's a partition between the bays I can lower."

"Perfect." Officer Frazier scribbled in her pad, then looked back up. "I'll go let my sergeant know."

I thought a moment. "Why not just park it at your lot?"

"There's a woman missing. Time matters. Besides, we can't let a vehicle with potentially live evidence sit out any more than is necessary. Looks bad in court later."

"Ah," I said.She stuffed her notepad back in her shirt pocket and clicked her pen. "Thanks again. If you point us to which bay we can use, we'll pull her in and let CSI get to work."

"Yeah, sure. Take that one on the end. It'll only need one partition to close it off." I pointed to the last bay in my bank of four.

"Perfect. Thanks, Sam," she said.

I shook her hand one last time, then watched her head back to her cruiser.

Officer Nuñez still hadn't moved. He was a statue.

"Was there something else, Officer?" I asked.

He reached up and removed his glasses, then he did the one thing I didn't expect.

He smiled.

And it wasn't the smile I'd expect from such a brooding beast, all full of fangs and drool. It was wide and warm; inviting. It extended all the way to his eyes, and I knew this guy was genuinely happy. It reminded me of a golden retriever when its human got home from work, all tail wags and tongue.

What the hell is he so happy about? I thought.

"No, I think we're good," he said. His voice was a rumble and carried a hint of someplace distant. His eyes lingered on mine, then roamed down to my chest and back up. "I just wanted to get a better look ... at things."

Holy shit. Did this cop just eye-fuck me?

My heart was suddenly racing like a teenage girl being asked to slow skate. I somehow forgot English.

"Uh ... sure. I mean ... anything in particular you need to see?" I stammered.

Nuñez's grin widened. "Nope. I'm seeing everything I wanted to right here. It's nice to meet you, Sam the mechanic."

Then the fucker turned and strode back to his cruiser, leaving me stunned and staring after him.

CHAPTER FIVE

SAM: SUNDAY FUNDAY (SUNDAY, JUNE 7, 6:45 P.M.)

I spent most of the next day rooting around Mrs. Polk's car. The shop was only open for a few hours in the afternoon on Sundays, but I was bored, and this car was seriously cool. Mrs. Polk's husband had taken incredible care of it. There was barely a hint of grime or dirt anywhere under the hood, which was almost impossible, given the car's age. Either they never drove it, or her husband had taken meticulous care of it throughout its long life.

Unfortunately, the transmission was beyond repair. I asked Tyler to find me a replacement, then called Mrs. Polk to give her an update.

As I hung up the phone, I glanced at the board to find there was nothing waiting for me in the garage. The guys were all busy, but there weren't any cars waiting in line. I leaned back in my squeaky office chair and propped my feet up on my metal school-teacher desk. My eyes roamed aimlessly, then landed on a business card with a blue shield embossed across the top. I hadn't really looked at it when Officer Frazier handed it to me, so I picked it up and gave it a quick read.

Frazier's smile and blonde hair popped into my mind, then her hunky partner shoved her out of the image and smiled down at me. Unruly brown hair sprouted from beneath a crisp blue cap with POLICE embroidered in silver thread. The sleeves of his uniform were rolled up, barely containing his thickly muscled arms. A faded tattoo I couldn't quite make out snaked around and down one bicep. Deep, chocolate eyes drank me in—or I drank *them* in—I kind of got lost for a minute.

And just like that, I popped a boner in my coveralls.

Great. Just great.

I tried thinking of Mrs. Polk. Nothing killed a boner like a little old lady, but Officer Nuñez had no respect for the elderly and shoved her out of the way just like he'd done his partner.

How rude.

And totally hot.

Why am I daydreaming about that cop? I chided myself.

But I wasn't just hard, I was twitching, and heat was crawling up my chest into my neck. My hand found my cock pressing against my jeans. The way I'd started to sweat told me something had to be done, pronto, but there was no way I could take care of business sitting in my office. So, I reached for my phone and called the one person who always came through, so to speak.

"Hey, handsome," a warm voice wrapped in a Tennessee accent drifted through the receiver.

"Hey, yourself. Up for some company?"

Joe and I had met a while back at a house party. I think we talked for all of a minute before sneaking down a hall-way. That night ended with me shoving him up against the bathroom wall and pounding him back into the eighties. It was a good night.

We hooked up every couple months since.

I liked Joe, maybe more than I was willing to admit, but we kept things strictly above board. 'Up against the boards' might be a better way to describe it.

I could practically hear Joe grinning through the phone. "My place in an hour?"

"You got it."

I opened the door and strode into Joe's apartment. We were years past the knocking stage.

"Hey!" he called from his bedroom. "Come on back."

Joe was leaned up against a bank of pillows. He wore nothing but a pair of tartan-patterned boxers and a pearly white grin. My hard-on had died on the drive over, but his pale athletic body revved my engine all over again.

"How was your day, dear?" He was such a smart ass.

"It's about to get a lot better."

He leaned forward and rubbed his chest. "Stay over there. I want to watch you take off your clothes."

"Oh, you do?"

"Unbutton your shirt—slowly," he instructed.

"Bossy bitch." I grinned.

I liked this new game. He wasn't usually the one giving the orders. I reached up and teased open the top button, then the second. When the last one popped free and I started to slip out of it, Joe held up a hand.

"Don't take it off yet. Just open it a little for me. I want to see your chest and abs."

Slowly, I spread my shirt back.

Joe started rubbing himself through his boxers.

"Now, slowly, pull it over one shoulder."

I did, and he gripped himself and groaned. Then he scooted forward, yanked my shirt off, and tossed it in the corner.

"That was so hot, but I don't have the patience to unwrap my present. Get over here and fuck me," he ordered.

"I think I like you in charge." I leaned down and nipped his neck.

He grabbed my jeans and ripped the zipper down. Thick brown bush exploded out of the now-opened denim.

"Fuck," he said as his fingers found their way down the trail.

I squirmed the rest of the way out of my jeans and nearly toppled over as his mouth wrapped around my cock. "Hungry tonight, aren't ya?"

He grunted something through a full mouth.

His hand gripped my balls and the base of my dick, and I felt my tip slap the back of his throat. I grabbed his hair with both hands and shoved him further forward until he gagged.

He loved it rough.

So did I.

Spit dribbled down my cock and his chin as he slurped and slid with his hand and mouth. Just when I thought he might get me close, he pulled back and planted a slobbery kiss on my mouth. I devoured him, our tongues dancing a well-rehearsed ballet. His fingers gripped my arms, then dug into the thick fur covering my chest. I grabbed his head in both my hands and held his face.

My eyes peeked open and caught him gazing at me as we kissed. Something deep inside me stirred in that glance. I reached for the feeling, but it was like trying to grasp fog, vanishing before I knew what it truly was.

I discarded all thought and poured myself into our kisses. Joe's hard-on escaped through the slit in his boxers and pressed against me. Warm pre-cum covered his head, sending shivers through me every time he slid it against my cock.

Our lips never parted as he reached down and tore his undies free.

I slickened a finger with his moisture, then reached around him and teased his hole. He arched back and groaned again. He clenched and released, so I pressed further. His ass gripped my finger, and his hands flew up and kneaded my shoulders.

"Enough of this. You belong to me. I want your ass now," I growled.

His eyes flew open, but he didn't speak, just flipped over on all fours and shoved his beautifully rounded butt into the air.

I trailed my fingers down his hips, across the flesh of his ass, then gripped each side and spread him apart.

He squirmed.

"I'm gonna fuck you all night."

"Uh-huh," came the muffled reply, his face buried in pillows.

I leaned down and gently nibbled each cheek, then teased his hole with the tip of my tongue. Our bodies were now coated in sweat. The musky scent and taste of his pre-cum made my pulse quicken.

I couldn't be gentle anymore, couldn't hold back, so I drove my tongue deep into his hole. He arched higher as he stroked himself. I knew he loved the feel of my whiskers, so I shook my head back and forth to scratch the sides of his ass, then speared him with my tongue again … and again.

His body tensed, so I grabbed his wrist and pulled it away from his cock.

"Oh no you don't. Not until I say so."

He groaned again, then lifted his head from the pillow. "You're killing me, Sam. Damn."

"Sit up on your knees and put your hands on the wall like you're under arrest."

"Fuck, arrest me."

I chuckled. It wasn't exactly a role play, but it was still a hot thought.

He scooted forward and did as I asked.

I wrapped my arms around him and pressed against him, shoved as much skin against skin as I could, until sweat covered me. My cock teased between his cheeks, the shaft sliding up and down without letting the head slip down near his hole. He pressed back against me, his butt begging me to take him.

While kissing his back, I reached down to the night stand and grabbed a condom and rolled it on, then squirted lube into my hand.

Fuck it, I thought, and squirted lube all over his back, smearing it over his shoulders, then down his arms.

He chuckled, so I squished more into my palm and lathered his chest until every part of him glimmered in the lamp light. I gripped his cock and it was harder than I had ever known it. It twitched in my hand, pulsing as I squeezed and released.

"Fuck!" Joe shouted.

I tossed the bottle down, then pressed myself against his slippery body. I laced my fingers with his against the wall, then dragged my teeth against his neck. He leaned back and moaned.

No longer gentle, no longer teasing, I squeezed his fingers and shoved myself inside him. Our bodies rose as one. We moaned as one. We rocked as one. He pressed his head against the wall and I shoved him harder, slamming every ounce of strength I had into his tight, slick hole. He shouted into the wall, and I thought I might've gone too far.

"Don't you fucking stop, Sam Prescott."

So I didn't.

I grabbed him around the waist, tossed him onto the bed on his back, then grabbed his legs and threw myself back into him. Sweat now poured down my face and chest. Fire and hunger drove me into him, and I grunted with every thrust. He started to grip himself, but I slapped his hand away and wrapped his cock in my own slippery paw and jerked him hard.

I was *so* close.

His body tensed, and his abs clenched.

I shoved myself deeper and harder, squeezed and stroked.

"Oh, shit! Shit, shit, shit!" he shouted, just as his cock shot all over my chest, nearly reaching my chin.

I didn't last much longer, filling the condom and falling over on top of my sweaty, messy man.

⋘◆⋙

"That might've been the hottest sex ever," Joe said, looking up as I padded into the bathroom to clean up.

I glanced back with a lopsided grin. "Yeah, you were alright, I guess."

"Fuck off," he said through laughter.

A few minutes and a shower later, I stepped back into the bedroom with a white towel tied around my waist. Joe's eyes roamed my body.

"Careful with those eyes. I just cleaned up."

"It's all your fault, walking in a towel, showing all those nipples and stuff."

"Nipples and stuff?" I laughed. "You sure you're the smart one in the campaign?"

His reply was a pillow hurling across the room.

I sat on the edge of the bed with my clothes gathered beside me. I wasn't sure why I didn't just get dressed and leave like I'd done a hundred times before, but something held me there.

"You okay?" Joe asked.

I turned around and sat facing him.

"Yeah. I'm good. It's just ..." I looked down at my hands. "You want to have dinner sometime?"

When I braved a glance back at him, his mouth was open but nothing was coming out.

"I mean, we've known each other for, what, two years? Three? You're the only guy I've slept with in all that time, yet I barely know you."

Joe's mouth finally worked. "You mean like a *date*?"

"Uh, yeah, I guess so."

"Huh."

My eyes found my hands again. "That wasn't exactly the enthusiastic answer I'm used to—or was hoping for."

"Sam, I'm sorry. I didn't mean ... you just caught me off guard. Sure. Dinner would be great."

Joe never fumbled with his words. Words were his thing. I must've really thrown him.

"How about tomorrow night?"

He hesitated another second, then said, "Sure. Sounds good. Wear something pink and frilly for me."

I laughed and smothered him with the pillow.

CHAPTER SIX

SAM: FRIEND ZONE (MONDAY, JUNE 8, 12:35 P.M.)

"Ty, I just don't get it." I scratched the top of my head, then slumped back. We'd been sitting in a booth at O'Charley's for nearly two hours.

"Maybe he's into that guy he's working for, you know, the congressman with the big arms and butt that could—"

"I know who David Reese is, thank you very much. Joe thought he was an ass—a hot one, but still an ass."

"Well, were *you* an ass?"

I coughed a laugh through the beer I was nursing. "No, I was a perfect gentleman."

"As you slammed him into walls and threw him onto tables."

"What can I say? He likes it rough."

"Maybe you weren't as good as you thought?" Tyler quipped. "Did he ever say anything like, 'Is it in yet?'"

"Ha ha. Very funny." I tossed my napkin across the table. "I guess ... I don't know. That's what's so confusing. It *was* good. He kept calling and wanting more, for over *three years*. Then, all of a sudden, when I wanted to actually get to know him, he just shut down. Who does that?"

"I'm sorry, boss. That sucks."

"Yeah."

The waitress refilled Tyler's tea and offered me another beer. He waved her off, and she disappeared to retrieve the check.

Tyler took a sip, then glanced over his glass. "Did you really like him?"

I started to answer, then looked down. I drained the last of my beer, then slid it to the center of the table.

"I think so. Maybe. I don't know, Ty. I've never dated before."

Tyler leaned forward, his elbows now planted on the table. "Seriously? You're almost thirty."

I smirked. "You calling me old?"

Tyler grinned. "You do act like my grandpa half the time."

"Shut the fuck up, asshole."

The waitress appeared and set the check on the table. "Good to see you boys smiling again. You looked so serious."

"Thanks," Tyler said, dropping cash on the table. When I reached for my wallet, he waved me off. "Oh no, this round of therapy was on me. Besides, you were about to tell me a sad story about a boy who never dated."

I rolled my eyes, then looked out the window. Rather than the parking lot I knew was there, I was transported to a place at once familiar and foreign. Fields of gold and tan rose and fell over rolling hills. Cows and sheep roamed in the distance. There wasn't a building or road, not even a power line, anywhere in sight. It was beautiful and peaceful—and empty. Something tugged in my chest as I watched the clouds sail by in the crystal sky.

I shook myself free of the memory and the dingy parking lot resolved in my vision. "There wasn't exactly a wild gay community in the middle of Wyoming, unless you count the two male horses we caught humping one day."

Tyler nearly spat his tea. "What?"

I nodded. "My dad nearly fell off the Rover laughing."

"Shit, and they have massive—"

"You have *no* idea. When they get hard—"

"Please tell me you didn't go around looking at horse cock—or that it set some unattainable standard in your mind ..."

I grinned and shrugged. "You work with what you have, my friend."

"Sweet baby Jesus."

"Let's stick to guys." I laughed. "I opened the garage a few weeks after moving here. Since then, it's been all work. Joe was my ... outlet. He was great, but I wouldn't exactly call fucking every few weeks a serious relationship."

"No, definitely not. Although, I gotta admit, I'm a little jealous. It does sound hot."

"It totally was." My eyes drifted out the window again. "And he's a good guy, real stand-up, and nice."

"Shit. You *did* like him."

"Guess so. Yeah. I don't know."

"Well, it's time you moved on, my friend—and it's time I got back to the shop. You might have the day off, but my boss is a prick when I'm late." Tyler winked, stood, and stretched his back. "What about that cop?"

My head snapped up. "What about him?"

"Come on, man. I saw how you looked at him. You practically ate him with your eyes. And, unless my Spidey sense is completely off, he was doing the same to you."

I grunted. "He kinda caught me off guard. One minute we're talking about a missing woman and her car, then next he's—"

"Flirting?"

"Something like that. It was more a flirt hit and run." I shook my head. "I don't even have his number."

"You could call his partner."

"What the fuck, Ty? Just call her up and say what? That I thought her partner looked hot in his tight uniform and I'd like to suck his cock?"

He rolled his eyes. "That's one route. I was thinking more like asking if he has a boyfriend and letting her reaction tell you where to go next."

I crossed my arms. "You're nuts, you know that?"

"Yes, m'lord. As you say, m'lord." He gave me his stupidest grin and inclined his head like he was some medieval knight. "It might be your day off, but I have a line of cars waiting on my magical hands, and my boss is a real horse's cock."

"Magical hands," I snorted. "That's what got me into this mess."

"I'm pretty sure your hands weren't the body parts Joe thought were magical."

CHAPTER SEVEN

MIGUEL: THE PURSE (TUESDAY, JUNE 9, 10:23 A.M.)

I flipped through the victim photos while Donna scribbled notes on a legal pad. We sat in one of the precinct's interview rooms, rather than an office or conference room, because the space always made me think better.

"Okay, there was a lot of blood in the back seat, but only a little on the ground. Why would the killer care if blood trailed into the woods? It was a remote, restricted area. It's not like a ton of people would wander by to see it. Why go to the effort to tie a plastic bag on her head?"

Donna glanced up. "Biel said she was struck multiple times in the side and back of the head. He thinks it was personal; angry. The bag could've just been the killer minimizing the blood ... or maybe it shows something deeper, like shame or regret?"

"Interesting. You got all that out of a grocery bag?"

"It's just a guess."

"Makes sense though. The act of covering up showing remorse."

"Remorse might be a tad strong for someone who just smashed another person's head to pulp, but yeah, that's the idea."

"You're really good, you know?"

She shrugged again. "I like the psych side, trying to figure out what makes perps do what they do, how they tick."

"You're gonna make detective and leave me, aren't you?"

Despite the grim conversation, the edge of her mouth quirked. "Aww, sweet cheeks, I'll never leave you."

"Uh-huh. They'll wave a gold badge under your nose and you'll be gone. I'll kick your ass out of our cruiser."

She laughed. "I'd love to see you try. You might be big and strong, but I'm scrappy."

"Scrappy. I love it. You're *definitely* scrappy."

We turned back to the photos and our smiles faded. A minute later, she tossed pictures of the inside of the Shales' home onto the pile.

"You believe him?" she asked.

I looked up and cocked my head.

"The husband, do you believe him?"

We'd spoken with Karl Shale several times since Emily's disappearance, each conversation lasting more than two hours, as we tried to verify information and calm the frantic man.

"Hmm. You don't?" My metal chair squealed as I sat back.

She crossed her arms and scowled. We'd been partners since I joined the force, and I knew every expression she had to offer. She hated it when I answered her questions with a question. I couldn't stop a grin from forming.

It drove her even crazier when I smiled during a serious situation.

I chose the healthier path and didn't tease. "I don't know. He seems genuinely upset, like you'd expect. His story checks out so far, and CSI didn't find anything in the house."

"Yeah, I wasn't expecting much from that search."

I glanced down at the photos, pulling out one of the entrance to their house. "The only thing that bothers me are the scuff marks around the door."

Now it was her turn to cock her head.

"Look here." I flipped the photo around as she leaned across the table. "There's no forced entry. No damage to the door or jam at all. The only sign of any struggle are those scuff marks there ... and there."

"Shale says those have been there for months." She flipped through her pad. "He said that happened when movers dragged a new server into their dining room. The thing looks like it weighs a ton."

"Yeah." I nodded. "That's what he said, but did you notice the feet on the server?"

Her head snapped up, and she gave me her 'you're on to something' look.

"They're wide at the top, but split into two pieces that sit on the floor." I made a V with my fingers and pointed it down to mimic the feet. "I'd think skid marks would look more like lines than wide scuffs."

"Huh." She picked up the photo and held it closer. "Maybe. It's worth another look."

"Other than that, I don't see anything pointing to him. There's been no weird bank or credit card activity, his social media is all about begging people to help find her, and the one public appearance he did with local news was believable. Maybe the crime scene guys will turn up something from the car. That's our only real lead at this point."

She nodded absently.

"What?" I asked. "I know that look. You're not buying it."

"I don't know. Everything you said makes sense, but something about the guy just doesn't feel right." She slumped back. "And if she left to run errands, why don't we have any witnesses who saw her shopping—or whatever she was going to do? We've checked out every store she'd normally shop at and plastered her face across the news, and not a single witness has come forward from the day she went missing. There's no credit card activity, no checks written. Nothing."

"Did the tech guys get anything off her cell?" I asked.

"That's another thing," she said, standing and getting louder. "Shale said he found it in her purse when he tried calling her. Why would she leave her phone at home? Who does that?"

I shrugged. "It's weird, but I've forgotten mine—"

"No, it's not just weird." She snapped her fingers, leapt to her feet, then bent over the table and shuffled quickly through the photos, stopping at one showing the front seats of Donna's car the day it was found. "That's what I thought. How the fuck did we miss *that*?"

I glanced at the photo where she pointed. After a few seconds of staring, I looked up and shook my head, not seeing whatever she intended.

"*Her purse.*"

"There's no purse in the picture. What about it?"

"That's my point. It's not there."

She snatched up the picture of the foyer I'd just been looking at and pointed to a table by the front door.

"When we met her husband the first time at the house, there was a purse on that table. I noticed it because it was one of those expensive designer bags. See, it's right there in the damn pic." She tapped her fingers together. "What woman leaves the house without her purse *and* her cell phone?"

I really wanted Donna to be on to something. We needed a break, but this felt thin.

"Rich woman like that probably has a dozen purses—"

"Wait! Why didn't I think of this before?" She was suddenly animated. "We've got to get back to the house. If her billfold is in that purse—"

"Okay, you'd have something solid then, at least enough to get a search if Shale refuses to let us back in."

We made a quick call to Karl. He wasn't home but agreed to meet us at his house the next day.

—◆—

Wednesday, June 10, 1:15 p.m.

"Mind if I record our conversation? I can't read my own writing when I take notes during an interview." I gave him a sheepish grin and showed him some illegible scribbles in my notepad. I was sure Donna was suppressing a hard eye roll behind my back, but she knew my overly friendly routine opened people up in ways the stern cop act sometimes didn't.

Flies and honey, baby. Flies and honey.

He nodded. "Yeah, sure. Whatever you need."

After a few rudimentary questions we'd dreamed up in the car to make him comfortable, Donna stood and strode casually about the living room. Karl tried to keep his attention on me, but his eyes glanced up a couple times as she moved about.

The home was open-concept, and most areas, except the bedrooms and bathrooms, were visible from any point in the main area. Donna worked her way from the living room to the foyer. Karl finally broke eye contact with me and watched Donna with interest.

"Mr. Shale, would you mind if I looked through some of these items?" she asked while leaning over the table by the front door. Her back was to us, and she didn't turn.

"Uh, sure, I guess," he answered.

From where we sat, we couldn't see what Donna was looking at, though I knew she'd move quickly to the purse we'd seen as we entered. It still sat exactly where she'd remembered seeing it before.

I asked Karl a few more questions to keep his focus on me until Donna returned and sat beside me. In one glance, I knew she'd found something.

We thanked Karl for meeting us at short notice and assured him the department was working hard to find out what happened to his wife.

As soon as the car doors slammed shut, Donna muttered, "Her billfold was in the purse."

I started the car. As we pulled out of the driveway, she turned to me.

"Her *keys* were in there too."

CHAPTER EIGHT

MIGUEL: THE SEARCH (WEDNESDAY, JUNE 10, 1:15 P.M.)

I could barely keep up with Donna when we got back to the station. She marched past our conjoined desks straight to Brandt.

"Sarge, we need to get CSI back out to Shale's house," she said before he could look up from the coffee he was sipping.

"Hi, Sarge. Got a minute? We're not interrupting, are we?" He scowled as his gaze darted between us. "Doesn't that sound more pleasant and respectful when barging into a superior's office?"

"Oh, fuck off, Brandt," she said without missing a beat. If I'd said that, he would've likely thrown a stapler at me, but he had a soft spot for Donna. It didn't hurt that she solved more cases than anyone else in our unit. She really was a rising star who made him look good, and that bought a special amount of leash, even from Sergeant Crusty.

Brandt rolled his eyes in my direction, then pointed his coffee mug at me. "I blame you, Nuñez. Whatever comes out of her mouth, you own it."

I held up both hands like a perp surrounded by pointed guns. His glare felt like that sometimes.

"Boys, can we focus here?" Donna said with an air of command. "We need to hit the house again."

"Take a breath. I heard you the first time." Brandt dropped his pen onto a stack of paperwork and sat back. "Why?"

Donna filled him in on the photos, then our visit to the house where we found Emily's purse, billfold, and keys.

"Well, shit. Her keys too?"

We both nodded.

"Sounds like our loving husband just made the list." Brandt grabbed his pen and scribbled on a pad. "Alright, but we need a warrant this time. I don't want to ask for consent again. It'll just tip him off that we're onto something."

"Won't that happen the minute CSI shows up waving a judge's order?"

He nodded. "Yeah, but you know the game. It'll be too late for him to tidy up at that point. You two will end up babysitting while Detective Biel and CSI do their thing."

"How long do you think for the warrant?" Donna asked.

Brandt shrugged. "Case is high priority, and the prosecutor's office will move fast, but the men in black are slow these days. It'll probably take two, maybe three days. Write everything up, and I'll get it moving through the machine."

"Three days? Shit." Donna wasn't happy.

"It is what it is. Now, get Smiley out of my office. I can't take the light off his teeth anymore."

"Hey, I didn't smile once in here." I feigned protest, then smiled so wide my cheeks pinched.

Donna snorted a laugh and grabbed my arm like she was walking a perp. I hung my head and tried not to make eye contact. No good could come of poking the bear.

CHAPTER NINE

SAM: A Second Visit (Thursday, June 11, 9:23 a.m.)

Tyler and I sat in my office, drinking coffee, my small TV quietly chirping in the background. It was still early, and most of the guys hadn't arrived yet. The shop was quiet.

"God, some mornings coffee just tastes better." Tyler squeezed his eyes shut and took another long sip.

"Late night?" I asked.

"Nah. Just kinda foggy this morning. What's on the calendar today? Anything interesting?"

I glanced down at the clipboard containing the open orders in the shop. "I should have the Bel-Air done today. There's a guy bringing in a bike. You love working on those."

"Yeah, give me that one. I need something fun."

I started to make a smart remark about his dating life, but a news report on the TV caught my attention.

"*... body of thirty-four-year-old Emily Shale was found in Edwin Warner State Park.*"

I grabbed the remote and cranked up the sound. The TV was suddenly magnetic as both Tyler and I leaned toward the screen. The peaceful beauty of forested sections of the park was shattered by flashing blue lights, bright yellow tape, and a handful of uniformed men and women milling about. The cameraman's zoom made it feel like we were actually on the scene, though I knew he had to be well back from the cordoned-off area.

"*... entire area of the park has been closed to visitors. Nashville police have confirmed this is now a homicide case, but would not comment on the cause of death or offer other details.*"

"Well, shit. Look who it is." Tyler pointed to one of the uniformed officers on screen.

I leaned across my desk to get a better view. Three officers stood at the edge of a clearing, chatting. I didn't recognize one, but the other two were unmistakable. Officer Frazier's blonde ponytail poking out of her official baseball cap gave her away. The bulging biceps beside her belonged to none other than Miguel Nuñez, the smiling cop who practically ate me with his eyes the last time I saw him.

"Damn, he wears those pants well," Tyler said.

"Yeah, he's pretty hot."

"Pretty hot? Fuck, you don't get out much, do you? He's damn sexy. And that smile is—"

I laughed. "You mean the one he never lets slip? Have you ever seen such a happy cop? It kinda gives me the creeps."

"Oh stop. You could use a little happy in your life."

"What's that supposed to mean?" I crossed my arms and sat back.

"Easy, cowboy." He held up both palms. "I'm just saying it might do you good to get out there a little. You've been awfully mopey since Joe ghosted you. Even a crusty gearhead like you deserves to feel good now and then."

"I'm doing just fine, thank you."

The news moved from murder to celebrity gossip, so I turned the volume back to background level. Tyler took that as a cue and stood.

"You really should get out more. You're a good guy, Sam. Whether you want it or not, I bet you'd make some other guy happy if you gave yourself a chance."

I tried to meet his eyes, but mine were suddenly fixed on my desk. "Thanks," I muttered. "I guess—"

"Stop guessing. Get out there. Fuck knows you're not getting any younger."

And with that, Tyler grinned his way out of my office. Asshole.

Stupid Tyler and his harping made me think of Joe. I could see his face, feel the warmth of his body against mine, taste his lips. In three years of mindless sex, I'd never really stopped to think about what, if anything, it all meant—until recently. Now it was all I could think about.

I tried telling myself it was all just screwing, meaningless fun between two willing, hungry, lonely adults. Shit, were we lonely?

We never really talked, unless barked orders and guttural groans counted as conversation. I'd thought those were among the top forms of communication. They sure felt good in the moment.

Then my mind decided to replay our greatest hits, but what it revealed surprised me. Sure, we were naked in every vision, but we weren't up against a wall or bent over the kitchen table. We were lying in bed, holding each other. I gently stroked Joe's hair, or he mine. He pressed a tender kiss to my neck and nuzzled beneath my chin. He told me about the campaign, his frustrating candidate, the media, his outrageous friend Pete, or a million other small things that, in hindsight, added up to a beautiful picture of his life. I told him about the shop, laughed about Tyler and his constant jibes, even opened up about life in Wyoming. I didn't talk about my family to anyone. I did with Joe.

Hell, we *did* talk. I'd never even noticed.

I missed that.

I downed the last of my now-cold coffee and stood to shake myself free of the memories ... and of Joe. We'd had a nice date the other night, if maybe a little awkward at first. I'd told him I wanted more ... and then, nothing. He hadn't called or texted since, which wasn't unusual—our booty calls were always pretty random—but the silence since our last conversation somehow felt more, I don't know, final.

Getting my hands greasy usually solved most problems.

Unfortunately, every time I shoved something back into place or wrestled with a stubborn part, I thought of Joe. Yes, that's twisted, thinking of shoving parts wherever, but it's where my mind went. I couldn't stop thinking about the guy—and that had *never* happened before.

My frustrated brain was saved by the bell—literally. The shop chime rang out, and all eyes turned to see the flashing blue lights atop one of Metro's finest cruisers pull up to our doors. I wiped my hands on a nearby rag and watched as Officers Frazier and Nuñez climbed out. She was shorter than I remembered. He was taller. Maybe seeing them side-by-side played tricks on my depth perception, but I swear the cops had stretched and shrunk.

I seriously needed a vacation.

Frazier was first to reach my bay's entrance.

"Sam, good to see you again," she said, extending a hand.

I held up my still greasy palm. "Happy to share the shop, but I doubt you want grease under your nails."

She smiled and pulled her hand back. "Good thought. Thanks."

Nuñez stepped forward and stabbed out his meaty paw. I didn't mean to raise a brow. It just happened.

"Grease doesn't bother me," he said. His voice was gravel in a bike's engine.

I didn't want to leave the man hanging, so I shook his hand. I swear he held it longer than was necessary.

Was he sizing me up? Was this some cop thing, reading a witness or whatever?

Then he smiled and something inside me lurched. I freed my hand and absently began wiping it again. I'd never seen such an interesting rag. It captured all of my attention.

Nuñez grunted a laugh.

Frazier's voice held a grin. "We're just here to check a few things out on the wreck. Crime scene guys tore it apart pretty good, but we want to see something for ourselves. Shouldn't take long."

"Alright. I saw the news this morning. Terrible about that woman," I said, fishing for some interesting insight.

"Yeah, definitely," Frazier said.

It was clearly all I would get from her, so I moved on. "Car's where you left it. Let me know if you need anything."

They were several steps away when I finally dared a glance. Nuñez's uniform looked even better on him from behind. Were all cop pants that tight-fitting?

"Damn, that's an ass." Tyler's low whistle snapped me out of my ogling.

"Hey, easy. They'll hear you."

Tyler chuckled. "Maybe I want him to. You can have her."

I rolled my eyes and walked around the car I'd been working on, a BMW whose owner claimed the A/C was about to die. It just needed freon. Things were rarely as bad as owners believed.

My bay sat beside the one we'd rented to the police department. Movement in the space between the BMW's opened hood and windshield caught my eye. Nuñez was focused on something in the engine compartment of the vehicle. I watched as he bent over to get a closer look.

He's comfortable under the hood of a car. Interesting, I thought.

When he straightened, his ass nearly ate the whole backside of his pants. I broke out in a sweat.

Damn.

"Our guys should be out with a tow this afternoon to take her off your hands. Now that this is a homicide, CSI will want the car in our shop."

I banged my head on the hood as Frazier's voice startled me out of my staring. Hand on head, I wriggled out from under the Bimmer.

"Uh, take as long as you need," I said. Shit, that hurt.

The grin on her face told me she missed nothing.

"He's single, in case you were wondering."

"What? No, I wasn't ... really ..."

She wheeled about and strode away, her shoulders bouncing as she chuckled all the way back to the cruiser.

Fucking cops.

Frustrated in every way, I did the only thing a self-respecting man could do in such a situation: I looked back to find Nuñez's ass. But instead of catching another glimpse of his uniform-munching cheeks, I found him watching me. His face brightened when he saw me look up, and he waved.

Like some teenager from across a playground, he actually *waved* at me.

We were twenty freakin' yards apart. Who does that?

So, being the mature, grounded, secure-in-his-masculinity type of guy that I was, I waved back.

Then the fucker gave me his best headlights-bright, all-teeth-and-no-lips smile. I swear the shop brightened in that moment. What the actual fuck?

"You should write a note and fold it into a plane and fly it to him. Maybe you can meet after class or trade juice boxes." Tyler must've been a cop in another life.

"Didn't I tell you to fuck off earlier?"

"You know I stopped listening to you a few years ago, right?" He grinned. "Go talk to him. If you don't, I will."

"Don't you—"

His shit-eating grin killed whatever I was going to say.

"Asshole."

"And you love me. Now, go talk to the hot cop."

"I'll think about it. Now go away and call this car's owner. I should have the A/C done in fifteen."

"Aye, aye, cap'n." He saluted with two fingers. I shook my head as I watched him vanish into the office.

"You two a thing?"

I nearly jumped out of my jeans.

"Jesus. Is sneaking up on people a thing with you cops?"

Nuñez crossed his arms. "Is there a reason you're jumpy, sir? Are you hiding something? Do I need to take you in?"

His suddenly serious tone threw me further. "Uh, no, not from you. I mean, no, I'm not. Really."

"Well, shit. I was hoping my handcuffs would fit."

The wrench in my hand clanged to the floor as my jaw dropped.

He burst out laughing.

Great. Now he knows I'm a twelve-year-old.

"Sorry, didn't mean to throw you off," he said, smoothing the amusement from his mouth. "I just wanted to let you know we're done. I expect the towing guys will be by later this afternoon to take her off your hands."

"Uh, thanks. Your partner told me. Uh, will your guys put her back together or do you need us to do that?"

He shook his head. "No, please don't touch anything. Our evidence team will bag all those parts up. Your guys don't need to do anything."

"Okay. Easy enough. I do nothing really well."

"I bet you do *some* things well too," he growled.

My face flushed, and I was sure my ears were as red as the Bel-Air's paint. I tried to look away, but his damn eyes were magic ... or something really hard to look away from. I was articulate ... in my head.

His grin morphed into an expression I couldn't read.

"Uh, so, was there anything else?" I asked.

"Yeah," he said. "There's one more thing, and this is vital."

He leaned in.

I mirrored him and leaned forward, expecting a whisper or secret code or some other twelve-year-old's spy book nonsense.

I sucked in peppermint mixed with strong coffee. It was heady.

Without dropping his gaze from my eyes, he dug into his chest pocket and pulled out two slim pieces of glossy paper, then whispered, "I have tickets to the Sounds game tonight. Want to join?"

"Sounds?" I said, barely able to connect my brain to my mouth.

"Yeah, you know, the baseball team."

"Uh, yeah, of course, baseball. Right. Uh, is this part of ... you know ... the crime thing? Hunt? Search?""Investigation?" His eyes were actually laughing. How was that even possible?

I nodded like an idiot.

"No, this is very much non-police business."

"Oh, sure, of course. Sorry, I just … never mind." Then the last two brain cells on duty clicked together. "You mean … a date? Really? Wow … uh, yeah, sounds great."

"You use big words. That's kinda hot." His grin widened to impossible, likely painful proportions. "I promise not to wear my uniform since it seems to mess you up, but I'll bring my handcuffs, just in case you're really bad."

And just like his partner, he didn't give me a chance to snap back. He just turned and marched back to the cruiser.

Fucking cops.

CHAPTER TEN

SAM: BATTER UP (THURSDAY, JUNE 11, 6:47 P.M.)

Summer nights in Nashville can be a bit like an armpit: hot, sticky, smelly, and wholly uncomfortable. There wasn't an ocean breeze to ease the heat, and the air often felt so thick you had to push through it as you walked.

For some twisted reason, I loved it.

I paced just outside the gate near the south entrance to First Horizon Park, home of the Nashville Sounds. Like an idiot, I'd worn a white T-shirt, which now clung to my body like a bikini on an ocean-soaked model. Even the blue logo looked drenched.

Miguel and I weren't supposed to meet for another twenty minutes, but I got there early. I'd never been to the stadium and wasn't sure how bad traffic would be. Miguel seemed like the kind of guy who was always on time. The last thing I needed was to show up to our first date late.

First date.

The very idea made me shiver. I couldn't decide if that was excitement, fear, dread, or some other emotion teenagers felt when meeting their note-trading partner after school. All I knew was that I was sweating my balls off in the heat, could barely breathe from stupid nerves, and I had to pee really bad.

My phone buzzed. Tyler's face appeared.

"Oh, boss, really? White?"

"Fuck off. I looked up the team's colors—"

His laughter stopped me short.

"You did *research* before your date? Aww, that's cute. Did you bring a corsage? Everybody going to prom wants one."

"You're a real asshole, you know that."

"The best." He finally stopped laughing. "Lower the phone. Let me see what you're wearing."

I did.

"Okay. Not bad. The jeans are nice and tight, but not squeezing the boys so bad we can tell your religion. But that shirt ... it's *so* white. Doesn't the phrase 'team colors' imply there *are* colors? And, well, your headlights are on super-bright. If that doesn't get your cop's engine going, nothing will."

"He's not *my* cop."

"Mm-hmm. Once he sees those nipples poking through, he will be."

"Ty!"

He laughed. "You look great. Just have fun and don't worry about what might or might not happen."

"Yes, Mom."

"That's *Dad* to you. Wait, no, you're definitely the daddy. Will you spank me? Pretty please."

"I'm hanging up now."

I shoved my phone into my back pocket.

A muffled "You have a great ass, but I'm suffocating back here" drifted up.

Shit, I'd forgotten to hang up. I laughed at Tyler as I pulled my phone back out and clicked the red end-call button.

"Something funny?" A familiar Harley purred behind me, and I nearly wet my pants right there.

"Shit. You snuck up on me again."

Miguel's ever-present grin widened as he shrugged. "I'm good at it. What can I say?"

My eyes roamed his royal blue jersey with Sounds scrawled across the chest. The S was a treble clef, a bit of club cleverness I'd learned from my pre-date research. I tried not to look down, but one glance at his jeans told me two things: one, he wasn't wearing underwear; and two, his jeans shattered Tyler's rule, clearly detailing his religious persuasion, or at least his parents' non-snipping one. His snake had a sweater—and holy cow, it was a python.

"I'm up here, sunshine."

"Sunshine? Oh ... uh ... sorry. You look nice. I mean good. You look great."

"You too." He reached out and squeezed my bicep. Heat bloomed in my chest, and I wobbled a little.

I'd never been one to get nervous, especially about a guy. Hell, I'd tossed Joe around his apartment enough to never be scared of a hot ass. But I swear I almost piddled at his firm touch. What the hell? Why did this cop turn me into a jittery mess? A quick check showed no evidence of *actual* piddle. *Thank you, baby Jesus.*

"Here," he said, holding out my ticket. "We've still got a few minutes before the game starts. Want something to eat? A beer?"

"Both sound great."

We made our way through the gate, then Miguel led me to a concession stand whose line was only a few people deep. My stomach rumbled as popcorn, hot dog, and hamburger aromas smacked me in the face.

"Eat much?" Miguel asked with a shit-eating grin.

"I get asked that a lot these days. What can I say?" I was determined to steer the conversation to safe ground and finally learn a little about this guy. "You seem like a real team fan," I offered, demonstrating my superb observation skills.

He smiled. "Yeah, you could say that. I got to know the team back when I played. When I moved up here from Atlanta to join the force, I bought season tickets. They're a fun distraction and make me feel like I'm still part of the game."

"You played? What, in high school? College?"

He nodded. "And in the minors."

"No shit."

"Yeah. It was pretty cool. Not as glamorous as people think, especially at that level, but I was living a dream."

Miguel spent the rest of our time in line filling me in on the team's history, lineup, and current standings in the playoff race. Two things became painfully obvious. First, Miguel loved baseball and the Sounds. Nobody could know that much about a minor league team and not harbor some deep passion for the game. Second, he was funny as hell. Every other statement about the team was accompanied by some quip or joke. He had me laughing all the way to our seats. That carried a double edge. On the one hand, I was really enjoying myself. On the other, my need to pee pinched my gut with every giggle. I was getting desperate.

"Okay, I know we just sat down, but I've had to pee since before you got here."

"Aww, did you pinch it off just for me?"

The dumbass made me laugh again. "You're such an idiot. I'll be right back."

"Save you a seat," he said, waving back at me like I was some lost relative. People sitting nearby eyed me, then snuck a look at him. I was pretty sure everyone knew the gay boys had arrived.

———◦———

Miguel scooted forward as the first batter walked up to the plate, knocked clay off his cleats, then struck out. The next two Sounds batters followed suit, not making contact once. The opposing pitcher was on fire.

"Well, this sucks," he said, slumping back as the Sounds took the field.

"You really are into this team, aren't you? Don't think I've ever known anyone so into a minor league team."

He shrugged. "Guess it's different when you played."

My head cocked like a confused golden. "How was it, playing pro ball?"

His grin returned. "The minors are a slog. All you do is travel, stay in cheap hotels, practice, and play. It's a lot more work than most people realize."

"It's probably cool being part of a team like that."

"Very. The guys become a big family, even the coaches. Minor leaguers don't have the crazy egos you'd expect from the big league guys. We were all still trying to prove ourselves and knew there was a lot to learn. Even the coaches were like big brothers and fathers. I miss all that."

"Aren't cops like that?"

He grunted. "Sort of, I guess. It's definitely a fraternity, but not in the same way. We rally together whenever another cop is in danger, and we're united in a common purpose, but there's not the same closeness like on a team. I guess part of that was how young we were back then too. Hell, I was just a kid trying to play in a man's league."

"How long did you play in the minors?"

"Only a couple years. I had a shot at the majors too."

His grin faltered, just a bit, at that last part.

"Really? Wow. What happened?"

"Some idiot handed me a badge."

I wasn't sure if this was another joke or if his downcast eyes said more than his words, so I waited. His lips pressed into a tight line, and his eyes drifted out past the outfield. I could tell he wasn't watching the game, but remembering ones from the past.

Unsure what to say, I pulled on my beer and munched popcorn. He startled me when he started talking again. His voice sounded distant and laced with ... *something*. Regret, maybe?

"My dad was a cop. His dad was a cop. My brother and sister are cops. It's kind of what we do."

"But major league baseball? That's a once-in-a-lifetime shot."

"Yeah. It was." He looked down at the grimy concrete beneath our feet, then his eyes rose and met mine. "It's hard to think about. I don't mind telling you sometime, just not here, okay?"

"Yeah, sure. Of course."

He tried to smile again, but the usual brightness in his eyes was missing.

The third inning came and went. Miguel pointed to players and quoted stats. The Sounds had finally started hitting and were up by two runs. It was strange to think of the game as a distraction, but it was a welcome one that snapped Miguel out of his momentary funk. I liked seeing his smile return.

When the fifth inning rolled around, our three beers were again torturing my bladder. Miguel made some smart-ass remark about how dainty I was, but offered to stretch his legs and walk with me.

"So, a brother and sister? Just the three of you?" I asked as we wedged ourselves back into our seats.

He nodded. "Yep, just us. My brother is the oldest. I'm the forgotten middle child, and Laura, my sister, is the spoiled baby."

"Wait, you're not the spoiled one?"

For a second, it looked like he thought I was serious, then he laughed. "Very funny. Glad to see you know how to give it too."

"You have no idea," I muttered under my breath.

"Oh really now?" The fucker had heard me. Both brows raised, his smile morphed from laughter to something far more heated.

"Uh, well, I—"

He reached out and patted my leg, sending shockwaves up my spine. "It's alright if you open up to me. I'm a cop. I crack nuts for a living."

I had no idea what to say to that.

He laughed again, a wave of fire flaring up my neck.

"Keep blushing like that and I might have to try my nutcracker on you."

I fumbled with my popcorn and white fluffs flew all over the old lady in front of us, falling into her lap and sticking in her hair like she was made of glue. My blush-fire turned into a three-alarm blaze, and Miguel doubled over, the last of his composure completely gone. Tears streamed down his face.

"I am so sorry, ma'am," I said, as I gingerly picked popcorn out of her perm. The darn things should've been slick with butter, but every piece clung to her hair like a drowning man to a lifeboat. She grabbed a few pieces that had fallen in her lap, turned, and tossed them back at me.

Miguel was now gasping for air.

"It's okay, honey. I'm just enjoying listening to him embarrass you all night. With sparks like that, I bet you get some before it's all over though. He's a tasty dish. If I was thirty years younger, I might have to try him out for myself. Although, I think I'd be the one cracking nuts in that case."

Her eyes darted to Miguel, then she started cackling, while Miguel practically hyperventilated. I wanted to crawl under the stupid stadium seats.

"Annie, you're the best. Enjoy that free popcorn." Miguel leaned forward and gave the old woman a peck on the cheek. She dutifully plucked a piece out of her hair and popped it in her mouth.

"Mmm. Extra butter." She winked.

When Miguel turned back to me, my mouth was open wide, but words wouldn't work.

"Annie and I have the same seats every year, have had for six seasons. She's the coolest chick you'll ever meet."

"Chick?" My eyes darted to her gray hair still littered with popcorn.

"Love you too, Smiley," Annie said without turning around.

Miguel winced.

"Smiley?" I asked, sensing Annie had just tossed me a little ammo to level the field.

"It's the nickname the guys gave me in my rookie year in the minors. It only took one cop in my academy class for it to stick. Half the force doesn't even know my real name now."

"I like it. You're a pretty rugged guy, and it's, well, kinda cute." I couldn't suppress a grin of my own.

"In a job that's filled with some pretty grim shit, being accused of smiling too much is a badge of honor to me." He shrugged, undaunted by my teasing. "My dad struggled. He ran the Major Crimes Unit in the years before he retired. I watched him go from one of the most outgoing, positive people in the world to a quiet recluse, haunted by images he'll never wipe from his mind."

"What would do that to a man with so much experience? Don't you become desensitized at some point?"

"Not really. If you knew some of the scenes we walked into … well, be glad you don't. My dad wouldn't talk about some of his cases, but there aren't many secrets in a police department—and we all saw the news. You can't hide the really morbid stuff, only the details that aren't released to the public."

"I can't even imagine." I watched Miguel's gaze again wander aimlessly across the field, seeing but not seeing the players and the game. "Sorry, didn't mean to get so serious."

He turned back toward me, and his smile returned. "It's life—our life, anyway. We chose it, so I guess we don't really have a right to complain."

We hadn't been paying much attention to the game and were startled when everyone around us began standing. We hopped to our feet as an organ blasted *Take Me Out to the Ballgame,* and Annie surprised me with her singing voice.

"Wow, Annie's *really* good," I leaned toward Miguel and whispered.

Annie, with ears like a wolf, whipped around and bowed dramatically. "Happy to perform for you boys any time."

"Annie sang on Broadway," Miguel explained.

My brows rose. "No shit. Oh, sorry. Excuse my French."

Annie chuckled. "Honey, I've heard it all—French, Italian, Russian, you name it."

I couldn't help but grin. Annie clearly had that effect on people.

"She's a living, breathing celebrity." Miguel winked, earning a girlish giggle.

Two innings later, the game ended with a whimper. Nashville led by seven runs going into the ninth, and most of the fans started drifting toward the exits as the first batter stepped up to the plate. Miguel grabbed our empty cans.

"Want to beat the crowd? It can be a pain getting out of here."

"Yeah, sure."

"I parked in the team's lot—the privilege of being a cop and working their games sometimes. Want a ride to your car?"

"That'd be great."

On the way to Miguel's car, I remembered the whole reason we'd met in the first place, and curiosity overcame good sense.

"I know you're probably not supposed to talk about your case, but any idea what happened to that woman? It's all over the news."

We walked a dozen or so yards before he glanced around us, then spoke quietly. "I can't say much. A detective took over as soon as this was ruled a homicide. We'll still work on the case, follow up on leads, that sort of thing, but the ball is his now."

"Need anything from us? Your guys got the car this afternoon."

He shook his head. "Nah. We got it."

When we reached Miguel's cruiser, he started to climb in, but I stood frozen on the passenger's side. His head poked above the hood.

"What?" Then he realized my confusion and laughed. "Get in the front. You won't be able to open the door if you sit in back. Then again, maybe that's not such a bad thing. I could keep you locked up."

I blushed. Being on the receiving end of handcuff and lock-him-up comments was new. I was usually the guy talking rough and dirty. Miguel Nuñez threw me totally off my game.

The funny thing was, I think I liked it.

When we got to my car, I reached a hand across the mounted laptop, as if we'd just concluded some business transaction. Miguel grinned and shook his head. He turned his shoulder toward me, reached out his hand, but didn't shake the one I'd offered. Before I knew what was happening, his fingers gripped the back of my neck and pulled me across the seat. A heartbeat later, his lips pressed to my mouth. His grip was firm, his kiss gentle and sure at the same time. I sucked in a breath and the heady taste of beer and popcorn teased my tongue.

He pulled back, but didn't let go of my neck.

"I had a great time, Sam the mechanic. I've got an early morning. Otherwise, I'd suggest we get ice cream or something.

"Ice cream? You mean, like after we go to the roller rink and do the slow skate?"

He barked a laugh. "Something like that. So, can I see you again?"

I couldn't pull my eyes away from his. He'd surprised me at every turn throughout the night, thrown me off balance with his humor and wit, and now he'd stolen my breath. Who was this man? This frustratingly confident, perpetually pleasant keeper of the peace?

Unable to form words, I nodded.

He smiled, then pressed his mouth to mine again. This time, there was no force, only the soft, gentle grazing of skin against skin. His tongue grazed my bottom lip as he pulled back.

I climbed out of the cruiser and started to turn, but the window rolling down made me look back. Miguel was leaned over his laptop, looking up at me with a pearly white grin.

"Have a good night, Sam the mechanic."

CHAPTER ELEVEN

MIGUEL: HOMEWARD BOUND (THURSDAY, JUNE 11, 10:17 P.M.)

I sat in my cruiser and watched Sam vanish into the sea of cars in the lot. Damn, he looked good in those jeans. I couldn't wipe the smile off my face. It had been a long time since a guy had done that to me.

My phone vibrated, so I grabbed it and unlocked the screen.

DONNA: SOOOO, HOW'D IT GO? YOU GETTING ANY ASS TONIGHT?

ME: VERY FUNNY. NO, THERE WILL BE NO ASS-GET-TING.

DONNA: PLEASE TELL ME YOU AT LEAST SAW HIS TITS OR DICK. SOME SKIN?

ME: NO. ABSOLUTELY NO SKIN WAS EXPOSED OR FELT OR ANYTHING ELSE. HE DID SPEW POPCORN ALL OVER ANNIE. THAT WAS FUN.

DONNA: THE OLD LADY WHO SITS IN FRONT OF YOU?

ME: YEP.

DONNA: WOW. HE'S GRACEFUL. SO ... NO SEX OR NAKEDNESS, NOT EVEN A LITTLE COPPING A FEEL, PUN INTENDED?

ME: NOPE.

DONNA: WELL, SHIT. I THOUGHT THIS ONE HAD POTENTIAL.

ME: HE DOES. THAT'S WHY NOBODY GOT NAKED.

DONNA: DAMN.

ME: WHAT?

DONNA: YOU LIKE HIM.

ME: YEAH, I GUESS. SURE. I DO.

ME: I CAN'T REMEMBER LAUGHING THAT MUCH IN A LONG TIME.

DONNA: WHAT ARE YOU TALKING ABOUT? YOU NEVER STOP LAUGHING, SMILEY!

ME: HA HA.

DONNA: SEE!

ME: FUCKTARD.

DONNA: I WANT DETAILS TOMORROW. OH, DON'T FORGET, YOU OWE ME.

ME: HUH?

DONNA: YOU NEVER WOULD'VE HAD THE BALLS TO ASK HIM OUT IF I HADN'T PUSHED YOU. THAT WARRANTS A DINNER OR SOMETHING NICE. I ACCEPT JEWELRY OR SHOES AS A SUBSTITUTE FOR FOOD.

ME: THE NUMBER YOU TEXTED IS NO LONGER IN SERVICE.

DONNA: DUMBASS. GLAD YOU HAD FUN. SEE YOU IN THE A.M.

I dropped my phone on the charging pad and cranked the car. There was an eternal line of cars at the exit, and I didn't feel like inching my way in that conga line. For a second, I thought about flipping on my lights and giving the good fans of baseball a scare with my siren, but the good cop in my head swatted down that idea. My laptop called to me, begging for work to get done, but I definitely wasn't in the mood for murder and mayhem.

Instead, I chose the route of any self-respecting high school boy who'd just left his first date and was determined to not look pitiful or desperate: I grabbed my phone again. My fingers had a mind of their own as they scrolled through my contacts and sent a text.

ME: YOU TASTE LIKE BAD BEER AND BUTTER.

SAM THE MECHANIC: NOBODY'S EVER SAID I TASTED LIKE BUTTER BEFORE. YOU'RE SUCH A SWEET TALKER.

ME: DON'T GET ALL MUSHY ON ME. I SAID BAD BEER FIRST.

SAM THE MECHANIC: IS THAT THE SAME AS COLD PIZZA? IT'S STILL PIZZA, SO IT'S AWESOME. I AM AWESOME, AFTER ALL.

ME: CAN'T A GUY PAY A SIMPLE COMPLIMENT?

SAM THE MECHANIC: OH, THAT'S WHAT THAT WAS. I THOUGHT IT WAS A MENU REQUEST.

ME: ONLY IF YOU'LL HAVE DINNER WITH ME :)

THREE DOTS DANCED ACROSS MY SCREEN. THEN THEY FROZE. A COUPLE SECONDS LATER, THEY WIGGLED AGAIN.

SAM THE MECHANIC: YES TO DINNER.

I slapped the steering wheel and accidentally blasted my horn. Several people walking to their cars startled and glanced back with scowls.

Me: And to dessert?

Sam the Mechanic: Ha. You better bring some damn good butter for that.

Me: I think you left all the butter in annie's hair. LOL

Sam the Mechanic: You're a very sick man. There has to be some kind of assistance program at the department for guys like you.

Me: They gave up on me years ago.

Sam the Mechanic: Clearly! LOL

Me: I really did have a good time tonight. Thanks for coming.

Sam the Mechanic: You miss me already. Admit it.

Me: Damn, you're cocky when you're texting. Where's the nervous little rabbit I met at the front gate? I swear you blush more than anyone I know.

Sam the Mechanic: Who says I'm not blushing right now?

ME: I'd love to see that.

Several seconds passed before the dots danced again.

Sam the Mechanic: Fuck, you're good at this.

ME: At what?

Sam the Mechanic: Making me feel like I'm twelve ... and making me smile.

Sam the Mechanic: Don't get me wrong. You're still an asshole cop.

ME: LOL That I am ... and maybe I like making you smile.

Sam the Mechanic: :)

Sam the Mechanic: Gotta drive now. Cops in this town are brutal on the whole texting while driving thing.

ME: For good reason. We want to keep you safe.

Sam the Mechanic: Aww. He cares about me. I'm all giddy.

ME: Who's the asshole now? LOL Go home. Talk tomorrow?

SAM THE MECHANIC: SURE … AND THANKS AGAIN FOR TONIGHT. I HAD FUN. GO SOUNDS!

I lost track of how long I sat in my cruiser staring at that last text. I'd faced hardened criminals, stood before countless judges and juries, dealt with cantankerous cops, and even battled top-notch pro pitchers at the plate—all of which barely made me sweat.

And here I sat, grinning from ear to ear, feeling ants dancing an Irish jig across my skin … over a damn boy.

I was so screwed.

CHAPTER TWELVE

SAM: POST-GAME REPORT (FRIDAY, JUNE 12, 8:21 A.M.)

S ome mornings, the coffee just doesn't brew fast enough.

"You planning to make love to that mug or drink it?" Tyler's far-too-chipper voice sounded from the doorway to my office.

"And a happy 'fuck you' this morning," I grumbled without turning around. Staring at the water streaming out of the coffee maker was far more interesting than the smug grin I knew was plastered across my closest friend's face.

"So, did the Sounds hit any home runs last night? Catch any fly balls? More importantly, did you get past first base with your cop?"

"He's not *my* cop," I snapped, a little sharper than intended. "And no bases were rounded ... or tagged ... or whatever you do with bases on a date. He's a gentleman."

The sound of the old pleather chair across from my desk creaking turned my head. Tyler had just planted himself and was squirming to get comfortable.

"He might be a gentleman, but I know you're a dirty bastard who likes to throw people against walls and bend them over tables."

I wasn't often speechless, but the early hour, lack of coffee, and Ty hitting a little too close to home had me thrown off my game. The drip finally stopped, and I filled my mug, then took a careful sip and savored the rich flavor.

"God, how can the same coffee taste so much better some mornings?" I thought aloud.

"Is the sun a little brighter? Are birds singing more sweetly? Do you hear Disney music in the background?"

"Didn't I tell you to fuck off?" I fell into my chair and threw my dingy boots onto my desk. "Fine. It was a good date. Feel better?"

I dared a glance over my mug to catch his eyes glittering a little more than usual. When I didn't offer any more, he leaned forward, pressed his elbows to the desk, and put his chin in his hands.

"Oh no you don't. Spill it. This is the first guy you've dated in, what? Four years? Joe doesn't count. In fact, his name shall be stricken from the record."

I grunted.

"Glad you agree. Now, speak, or I'll tell all the shop guys that you fucked in your office last night and to avoid touching any of the furniture."

"You little shit."

He beamed and batted his eyelashes.

I realized he wasn't going to let me drink my coffee in peace, so I set my mug on the desk and rubbed my eyes. "We went to the Sounds game."

"You? Baseball?"

"Shut it if you want to hear this."

He mimed locking his lips and throwing away the key. What a kindergartener. Why did I love him?

"We watched the game, drank too many beers, ate shitty food. It was fun." I waited to see if he'd let me off with that explanation, but he didn't budge. I sighed. "There was this old lady who sat in front of us. Guess she and Miguel have had season tickets for years and know each other. She had us cracking up most of the night."

"I ask about your date and you tell me about an old woman? I want a refund." He sat back and crossed his arms.

"Dude, really, there's not much to tell. We were at a baseball game surrounded by people. It's not like we could have a deep conversation or make out. He drove me to my car after the game, and that was that."

"Did you at least get a kiss?"

I hesitated.

"You did! Was it good? Did he come in all hot and heavy? Was he a torpedo tongue?"

"You are such a sick bastard. You know that, right?"

He laughed and nodded.

"It was ... surprising."

Now he quietened and his brow scrunched up.

"It was nice, not like I would've expected. I don't know. Cops seem all tough and rugged, but he was gentle ... tender."

"Oh shit." He uncrossed and leaned forward again.

"What?"

"Did he ask you out again?"

I nodded. "We're doing dinner tonight. I'm cooking."

"Damn. You're cooking on your second date? The day after the first one? You *really* like him."

It was a statement, not a question. My best friend just clocked the twelve-year-old inside me crushing on the new guy. Of course he did. Nobody knew me like Tyler. Great. He'd be relentless now.

I shrugged. "I guess, what I know so far. He's a nice guy, and he seems genuinely happy, not all serious like you'd think a cop might be."

"Uh-huh. You'd better put out before he loses interest. Maybe let him be in control. I know that's new for you."

"What—?"

"You know, let him toss you into the fridge or something. Wait, I know ... he has *handcuffs!* He could cuff you to the bed and do a deep interrogation, a full cavity search—use his big stick on you!"

I wadded a napkin and threw it at him. "Don't you have work to do?"

"Yes, boss. Whatever you say, boss." He laughed again and stood. "I'll save the blackmail about you sticking up the office furniture for something else now."

Before I could find something else to throw, he vanished into the shop, laughing all the way.

CHAPTER THIRTEEN

SAM: ROUND TWO (FRIDAY, JUNE 12, 5:43 P.M.)

"You're gonna be late." Tyler leaned against my office doorway, his arms crossed and foot tapping. Several new customers had shown up right as I was trying to leave, and I was doing some serious juggling to wrap things up. I grunted at Tyler without looking up.

"I can handle that for you, you know. They don't require the seal of the king."

I finally looked up to see both his brows raised and broad lines spreading across his creased forehead. I tossed my pen down and stood.

"All yours. Thanks, Ty."

"Whatcha gonna make for your cop?"

"He's not my—" I stopped when he started snickering. Asshole.

"Grilled chicken with teriyaki sauce, white rice, and steamed broccoli."

His face soured. "Holy shit. Are you going to work out with him afterward? Or are you just trying to impress him with a healthy meal?"

I grabbed my keys and started around my desk.

"I happen to like grilled chicken, thank you very much. Besides, it's the one thing I know I won't burn. You know me in the kitchen."

He laughed. "Yeah, true. It's probably best you go with the safe bet. Maybe he cooks. That would make you two—"

"There is no *us two*, Ty. It's just a date."

"Mm-hmm. Are you wearing those tight jeans you wore to the game? The ones that your ass eats, swallows, and digests every time you take a step?"

I tried not to laugh. The last thing Ty needed was encouragement, but it just rumbled out. "No, I was thinking something pink and frilly. Maybe chiffon with a tall hat and feather that blows in the wind."

"Oh, Sam. Don't you know it's not the feather's job to blow? It's *yours*?"

"I can't take you anymore. I'm outta here." He leaned back to let me pass. "Have a good weekend."

The shop guys turned at my shout. The fucker had pinched my ass as I walked by.

His laughter rang in my ears all the way to my car.

⸻◦⸻

By the time I fought Friday afternoon rush hour and walked into my tiny one-bedroom house in East Nashville, it was six thirty. Miguel was supposed to arrive at seven. I went into full holy-shit mode, tossing broth into a pot, whacking the white stringy stuff off the chicken, and cutting the trunk thing off the broccoli.

At six fifty-nine, there was a knock at my door.

An unfamiliar thrill ran through me, and the house was suddenly much warmer.

Did I leave an eye on too high? I wondered absently. I checked the stove as I ran to the door. The eyes were fine.

I skidded to the door in socked feet and peeked through the spy hole.

"Gonna let me in or just stare all night?" an amused voice called out.

I leapt back, startled, then reached out and opened the door.

Miguel wore a deep blue T-shirt and faded jeans. His shirt wasn't disco-club tight, but it hugged his chest and arms perfectly. His smile beamed when I opened the door and the flutter that started earlier bloomed into a full-blown butterfly parade.

He was so much hotter than I remembered.

"Hi," I said. One of my hands rebelled against adulthood and rose to wave, its fingers wiggling with just the right amount of girlish giggle to make Miguel actually giggle. Without a word, he raised a hand and mirrored my senseless welcome.

Then neither of us moved.

"Uh, can I come in?" he asked.

"Oh, yeah, sure. Sorry. I, uh, was just cooking and ... fuck, come in. Yes, come in."

English was suddenly my second, maybe fifth, language.

Miguel's eyes glittered, their corners turning upward.

"Smells good in here. What's for dinner?" he asked as we walked through the mudroom-style entryway into the kitchen.

"I went healthy on you. Grilled chicken, rice, and veggies."

"Yum. Sounds perfect." His other hand, the one I hadn't realized he was concealing, emerged from behind his back with a plastic grocery bag in tow. "I brought something to ruin your healthy meal."

I took the bag and pulled out a quart of mint chocolate-chip ice cream.

"Oh, you're evil. I could microwave this thing and drink it."

He chuckled. "It's my favorite too."

Without warning, he closed the gap between us, grabbed me with both hands, and pulled my body into his. I was so surprised that I didn't have time to resist his lips pressing against mine. My butterflies abandoned their parade floats and started gnawing my insides. It felt like fireworks bursting in my chest, begging to get out, to explode their colors into the kitchen.

The ice cream thudded against the floor. Neither of us looked down.

Miguel had my arms pinned against my sides, so I couldn't hold him back or struggle or anything else. The next thing I knew, he was walking me backward and pressing me against the refrigerator. His hands clamped around my wrists and pressed them above my head as he kissed me deeper.

A pot lid rattled, and he pulled back. I tried to say something, but breathing was suddenly a contact sport.

"I, uh, need to check on that. The rice. It's the rice, I think."

He leaned in and kissed me again, then pulled back and winked. "Guess you'd better check on it, then."

My knees were noodles, threatening to spill me all over the kitchen floor. I gripped the counter and regained my balance.

I was the one in charge, the aggressive one. I pressed guys against the fridge and tossed them onto the bed. I gave the orders.

Who was this guy and why was he taking control?

Why was I letting him?

And why the fuck did I like it so much?

My head shook slightly as I reached over and lowered the heat on the stove. Miguel had rattled me in ways no one ever had. The feel of his hard body shoved against mine, the heat of his breath, the taste of his lips, all of it swam in my mind as I stirred butter into the rice. I was self-aware enough to know I liked spending time with the guy and wanted to get to know him better, but damn, I had no idea how badly I would crave his touch. It consumed my thoughts as I passed him on the way to the porch to turn the chicken.

I snuck a peek from the grill and watched him wander about my kitchen and den, taking in the photos and prints on the bookshelves and walls. He looked like a man completely comfortable in his environment. Was he feeling any of the tornadic activity battering my insides, or was I the only teenager crushing all over himself? It would've been nice to see him just a little nervous, but something in his confident swagger made me swoon again.

Fuck me. Pull it together, Sam. You're a grown-ass man. Act like it.

The butterflies laughed in the face of my inner dialogue.

A few minutes later, dinner hit the table and we sat.

"Shit," I said. "Drinks. What would you like? I have sweet tea, Coke, beer, and I think there's white wine in the fridge."

"Beer's good," he said as I hopped up. "I like your place. It's cozy."

I snorted as I handed him a bottle of Corona. "It's small, but it's all I need."

"No dog? Cat? Hamster?"

"Hamsters are for power bottoms."

He spat the sip he'd just taken all over the table. "Wow. Didn't see that coming."

I grinned, finally gaining a hint of confidence. "I'm not opposed to cats, but dogs are the best. I'm just not here enough to be fair to a pet."

"Yeah, I know what you mean. I'm the same." He wiped beer off his arms with a napkin. "I miss having one though. The hiker who found that woman's car the other day had this golden, a big, fluffy, crazy-ass beast. It had to be the happiest dog I've ever seen. Guess it got me thinking about them."

He took a bite of chicken and made a groaning noise. "Mmm. That sauce is good."

I smiled triumphantly. "Took me hours to get the cap off the bottle. I'm a regular Chef Boyardee."

He grinned and shoveled another bite into his mouth like he hadn't eaten in days.

"Anything new on the case? You mentioned the hiker, made me think about it."

"Not really. We've got a few leads, but nothing solid. Once the CSI and lab guys finish their work, we hope to have more to go on."

"It's not like on TV, is it?"

He cocked his head.

"Solved in thirty minutes."

His chuckle was wry. "No, not at all. And we don't have fancy offices and crazy technology like you see on there. Most criminals make mistakes, but it can take a long time for us to find them."

"That's gotta be frustrating, especially when you know somebody's life might be at stake."

"Yeah. It's weird—and really terrible to admit—but the pressure was relieved a little when we learned the victim had been killed. I mean, I hate it. We wanted to find her alive, bring her home safe, but the intensity of an active search ... it's a lot."

"I bet."

I watched Miguel for a minute. Something in his face and the set of his shoulders as he talked about his work shifted. It was slight, barely perceptible, but it was there.

"How do you do it every day?"

He shrugged. "It's just what I do. It's what my whole family does. I guess you get used to it after a while."

I wasn't sure I bought that, but decided to give him a moment to eat in peace.

"What about your family? I know you have a brother and sister, both cops."

"Yeah, everybody's back in Atlanta. Dale is my big brother. I think he's thirty-four now. He's a mounty, trotting around town on more of a PR mission than anything to do with public safety."

"PR?"

"Yeah. Think about the past few years. It's been pretty rough for anyone in blue. I mean, bad cops deserve what they get, but the rest of us are just trying to do our job, to help people and keep them safe. Sometimes we need a little good press to win over hearts and minds. If horses can help, we're on them—literally."

"Huh." I hadn't ever thought about the police needing to market themselves. But in the aftermath of so many dying at the hands of overzealous cops, it made a weird sort of sense.

"Anyway," he started again after another pull of his beer. "My little sis is Laura. She's four years younger than me, and the smartest of us all. She'll be running Atlanta before it's all over."

When he spoke about his sister, his eyes brightened and his chest lifted. There was a pride where she was concerned that seemed special to Miguel. It was beautiful to see.

"What about your parents?"

"My dad's still in Atlanta. Mom died a while back, and he's never been the same. He hung in there, running the Serious Shit Division, as we called it, for several more years. I guess, after a while, he just couldn't take dealing with death and rape all day, then coming home to an empty house filled with memories of her."

The sadness in his voice made my heart ache. I didn't know what to say.

"It's okay," he said, reading my mind. "Nobody else knows what to say either. We're a cop family, bound by blue, so to speak. It's all part of the life, I guess."

We ate in silence for a long moment.

"Looks like the beer's getting low. I'll grab a couple more."

"Thanks," Miguel said, his smile barely lifting the edges of his mouth.

When I returned and set fresh bottles on the table, his usual good humor had returned.

"I thought you said you couldn't cook. This is great, Sam."

I rolled my eyes. "It's chicken, rice, and broccoli. Even a five-thumbed mechanic like me can't mess that up."

He took a swig of his fresh beer. "You don't take compliments well, do you?"

"Nope. Never have." I chewed a bit of chicken. "Come to think of it, I don't recall ever getting a lot of them. Maybe they just feel weird."

He cocked his head. "What do you mean?"

"I don't know. My family's fine. There were seven of us growing up, so it was easy to get lost in the middle of all that."

He whistled. "Damn. Seven kids?"

"Yeah. Good thing we lived on a ranch. We needed a lot of room, more for the kids than the cows."

"Where was home?"

"Wyoming."

"Ah," he said, as if that explained something.

It was my turn to cock my head.

"Nothing. Sorry. It's a cop thing. I can't help always looking for answers, even when there weren't questions."

I grabbed my beer again. "And what answers did you just find?"

He smiled. "Rural guy. Big family. Wide open space. Your parents were probably so busy just trying to keep up with all of you that you never really got that much attention, at least not individually. It would've been easy for your accomplishments to get brushed under the rug, or just missed in all the chaos. Plus, if my guess is right, you looked for opportunities to be out of the house, out in those open fields with your cows and dogs, or whatever else you had on the farm."

I waved my fork at him. "Ranch, not farm. Never a farm."

"Ranch boy, not farm boy. Got it." He chuckled. "Was I close to the mark?"

"Pretty darn close. You sure you weren't one of those telephone psychics in a former life?"

He laughed again. I was starting to really like that sound. It was warm and carefree, but rumbled from somewhere deep in his gut. It felt like an old favorite blanket you'd snuggle under while watching a movie on the couch.

What the fuck, Sam. He's a dude, not a throw. Where'd all that nonsense come from? I chided myself.

"I'm a cop. Reading people and figuring them out is what I'm trained to do."

"You're good at it. Gotta admit that."

He dropped his fork on his now-empty plate and sat back in his chair. "Where are your folks now? Your brothers and sisters?"

"All over the place. We're not really close anymore, at least not all of us. My baby sister and I are still tight. She's still in Wyoming, living with Mom and Dad. All the others are boys. Brian, the oldest, is a high school basketball coach near Murfreesboro. A couple moved out to California and got married, had kids, that sort of thing. Kevin, the one younger than me, kind of drifts. I'm not sure where he's living now. He'll pop up at random, usually around the holidays."

"Sounds like herding cats. Your poor parents ..."

I grunted agreement. "That's *exactly* what it's like. They're saints for putting up with all of us."

As I took the last bite of my chicken, Miguel tossed his napkin onto his plate and gathered his utensils.

"I don't think I can do ice cream just yet. Mind if we let this settle a little?"

"Yeah," I said between chews. "Sounds good."

We cleared the plates and got fresh beers, then headed toward the den. My place was tiny, but I spent serious money on my television and stereo. I flipped on the TV and a commercial for replays of *Lord of the Rings* was on. Bass nearly made the hardwoods vibrate.

"Damn, that sound is awesome," Miguel said. "And that picture. I don't think I've ever seen such a crisp screen. What is that?"

"OLED. It was the newest thing a few years ago. It's what your iPhone screen is made of."

"Shit, that's amazing."

"Yeah. I spent a few bucks on this setup. We could hunt for a movie?"

"We could," Miguel said. His voice carried a hint of mischief. "Or ..."

He closed the gap between us and grabbed me roughly by my hips, pulling me into him like he'd done before. I'd thought the butterflies had drifted away during dinner, but they'd just been resting up. All at once, they assaulted my chest and arms. Even the skin on my neck felt like they were clawing their way out with tiny, furry claws.

Miguel's hands were strong and firm, his grip sure, but this time, he hadn't captured my arms. I reached up and gripped his biceps, and squeezed.

Damn, they didn't budge.

"You like?" he said in a breathless whisper.

"God, yes. You feel really—"

He kissed me again and I forgot what I was saying. My hands moved around him, drawing our bodies together even closer, and I could feel his erection throbbing through his jeans.

"I have a better idea than a movie," he growled. "Unless you want to take things slow."

"I ... uh ... well—"

He pulled back.

"Don't stop."

"What was all that? You did want to take it slow, didn't you?"

"Are you doing that cop thing again?" I asked.

He grinned. "Sorry, can't help it. We can take things at any pace you want. It's just ... you're just ... damn."

I laughed. "It's about time you were the one stumbling over your words. You've had me throwing up on my shoes all night."

"Eww. Do you do that often? That might be a deal-breaker."

"Fuck off, asshole." I shoved his chest, and damn if it didn't budge either. My fingers massaged his pecs, and my eyes widened appreciatively.

"Or, we could toss speed limits out the window and see where things lead."

I looked up. His eyes were all hunger. Damn, he was hot, his body felt amazing, and I really liked him. Was I about to screw all that up? Were we supposed to slow down and wait for the third, or fifth, or some later date? I hadn't dated in so long I barely knew what I was supposed to do.

Miguel waited while my inner battle played out before him. His hands left my hips and found their way to the back of my neck. He leaned forward and pressed a kiss to my forehead.

What did that mean? My inner twelve-year-old panicked. *Was he disappointed? Should I just jump him right there, rip off his clothes, and*—

"Sam, I haven't dated in a while, and I really like you,"
he whispered. "The last thing I want is to mess this up."

My heart skipped a beat.

"But I really want to rip off your clothes."

Holy shit.

Then my mouth moved without consulting my brain.

"Do it. I like you too. Do whatever you want."

He didn't hesitate. Hands gripped the bottom of my
T-shirt and yanked it over my head faster than I could
think. By the time I'd realized the permission I'd given him,
we were both half-naked and I was pressed up against the
wall beside the television with Miguel's tongue halfway
down my throat. Both of our hard-ons had returned with
a vengeance, and he ground his against mine without mer-
cy, sending a shiver across my skin. I groaned through
tongue-locked lips.

Chapter Fourteen

SAM – Office Meeting (Saturday, June 13, 8:40 a.m.)

"Right there in your den?" Tyler leaned forward, a cat-that-ate-the-canary grin teasing his lips.

"Ty, it was so fucking hot. I could tell he worked out through his uniform shirt, but nothing prepared me for his naked glory. Fuck, he's hard as a rock—and ripped."

"Uh-huh. Let's get to the hard part. I want more rock and fewer ripples."

"You know how it was with Joe? I was the one tossing him around most of the time. Guess I like to be dominant in the bedroom."

"Or the den, or the kitchen, or the bathroom. Come to think of it, in your office too. You're a control freak."

"Very funny, asshole." I flipped him the bird. "Anyway, I never got the chance last night."

"What do you mean?"

"Well, shit, he grabbed me and shoved me against the wall before I could think. Next thing I knew, he was holding my wrists above my head. We made out like that, right next to *SportsCenter* blaring on my TV, for a good ten minutes. I tried to free my arms, but his grip would tighten and he'd smack them lightly against the wall, then give me this look."

"What look?"

"'Don't you fucking dare try to get away from me, you little criminal.'"

"Fuck, that's hot."

I nodded. "Not as hot as when he pulled out handcuffs."

Ty's mouth fell and his eyes popped wide. "What?"

"Yeah. I have no idea where he kept them. His jeans weren't that loose." I took a sip of coffee, more to gather myself from the mental image than anything. "*SportsCenter* had just gone off when he lowered my arms, let go of one, and spun me around with the other arm behind my back, like he was subduing a suspect. I thought my heart was gonna race out of my chest. I mean, I knew he wasn't gonna hurt me or anything, but it still scared the shit out of me."

"Shit, then what?"

"He spun me around toward the couch and clamped the handcuffs on the wrist he still held, then grabbed the other one and did the same. I stood there, in my den, arms locked behind my back, as Miguel slowly nibbled my neck with his tongue and teased my nipples with his fingers."

"Sweet Jesus."

"He moved around in front of me, never letting his fingers leave my body. That might've been the most sensual thing I've ever felt. Wherever his fingers grazed, a white-hot line seared into my skin. I lost count of how many times I shivered." I shivered just remembering. "And the look in his eyes—"

"What look?"

"Holy cow, Ty. It was out of some porn or fantasy or something. I don't know. He looked like I was the only person in the world and he wanted to devour me, swallow me whole. I mean, Joe and I had hot sex, but Miguel took passion to a whole different level ... and we still had our pants on!"

Ty stood up and paced my tiny office. "Don't stop there. You've got me all hot and bothered on a Saturday morning."

"Well, I was standing there, in the middle of my den, and he edged around in front of me, then sat on the couch and just looked up. His eyes roamed my chest, then abs, then back up to my face, like he was exploring every curve. Then he reached out, grabbed the top of my jeans, and pulled me toward him. His fingers tickled the hair—"

"I know which hair. Don't stop."

"By that time, my dick was soaked in pre-cum. He pulled his slick fingers out and licked them clean. I thought I was gonna either bust my load or pass out right there. Then he unbuttoned my jeans and pulled them down to my ankles, letting my cock pop free. I was so hard, Ty."

Ty sat again and leaned forward.

"He did that thing with his fingers again, tracing my skin across my abs, then my hip, then everywhere around my cock without touching it. My body kept twitching. I can't remember ever being so turned on without a guy touching my dick."

"Please tell me he touched it."

I nodded. "Oh yeah. He teased me so long I didn't think he was going to, but then he grabbed my ass cheeks in both hands and pulled me forward and shoved the whole length of me down his throat. I mean, shit, Ty, it was impressive. He didn't gag or anything—and I'm not little down there."

"I've heard, oh Great One."

"Ha ha." He got another bird for that. "Anyway, it didn't take long after that. I was so worked up that I came in like two minutes. As I got close, I tried to reach around, to pull him back, but between the handcuffs and his hands on my ass, I couldn't move. He swallowed me down and just kept going until I was totally soft again."

My chair seemed as satisfied as I had been, because it let out a long squeal as I leaned back.

"That's it?" Ty said, sounding disappointed.

"Yeah. He wouldn't let me touch him. Hell, I didn't even get to see him with his pants off. He said last night was all about me, showing me how much he wanted me."

"Okay, that's pretty sexy. I was thinking he had something to hide, like he was only packing an inch or two."

I laughed. "I'm one hundred percent sure that's not the case. Hell, when he ground against me, I could feel him. He's bigger than me. That should scare the shit out of me."

"You're all top. What difference would it make to you?"

"I don't know. I might, you know, for the right guy."

"Sam Prescott. Are you turning soft? For your cop?"

"He's not *my*—"

He held up a palm. "He sucked you senseless. Either he's yours or you *want* him to be."

I shrugged. "Maybe. I might. Fuck, I really like this guy."

I couldn't suppress a goofy grin.

"I can't believe I'm asking this. How was dinner?"

"Ty, it was great. It was like talking to somebody I've known forever— just easy."

"Red flags?"

That caught me by surprise. I thought a second. "I wouldn't say that—"

"But? I hear it in your voice. Out with it."

"Well, there was one point where he got really quiet. We were talking about his family, how they're all cops. He said something about his dad retiring and how the dark shit he saw on the job weighed on him, changed him. He got real quiet after that, but for just a few minutes."

"That doesn't sound like anything. Seeing murder every day has to take a toll."

"True," I said. "Do you think it's taking a toll on Miguel?"

Ty shook his head. "I don't know the guy, but he seems happy and stable, at least from what you've told me."

I nodded slowly, turning our conversation over in my head again. I wanted to believe that—I *needed* to believe it—but something nagged at the back of my mind, like I could feel there was something more, hidden under the surface.

CHAPTER FIFTEEN

MIGUEL—THE WARRANT (MONDAY, JUNE 15, 9:52 A.M.)

On Monday morning, Donna and I sat in my cruiser, coffees in hand. The application for a search warrant for the Shale house felt like it was taking forever. They always did. By the time we'd gathered enough evidence to justify a warrant, written up the details, and submitted them to the state's attorney, we were ready to go. Unfortunately, the system doesn't work that way. It slows things down for a reason: to double and triple-check things to ensure the state doesn't unfairly arrest or search—or anything—a citizen.

"System drag sucks," I said, taking a careful sip. The coffee was boiling.

"It is what it is. Gives us time to talk about you."

"Me?" I feigned ignorance. I knew exactly what Inspector Clouseau was after. She was brilliant, but was also pretty transparent.

"Out with it, Smiley. Your grin's been more ridiculous than normal this morning."

"What—" I tried to protest.

"Don't even try to act all innocent. You got some this weekend, and I want to hear about it. Now. Don't make me tase you right here in our car."

"Easy, tiger. I was just teasing." I laughed. "Donna, this guy's incredible."

She rolled her eyes and leaned against the driver's-side window. "Do go on."

"He cooked. It was pretty simple stuff, but good. But the conversation ... I don't know ... it just flowed. There was never a moment when we stared at each other and didn't know what to say. It felt like I'd known him a really long time."

"You're a cop, trained to get people to talk. None of this should be surprising. Get to the good stuff or I'm seriously reaching for my gun."

"You're so damn bossy this morning." I laughed again. "We didn't do *that*, if that's what you're waiting for."

"Why are you going all third grade on me now? Use your words. What did or didn't you do?"

"No sex. Well, no sticking tab A into slot B. I gave him a blow job."

Her brows raised. "That's it?"

I nodded.

"Did you get one? Tell me you got something."

I shook my head. "Nope, nada. Donna, I like this one. I'm not just saying that. I don't want to jump in the sack and ruin something that could be ... more."

"Oh shit. You're whipped. My little puppy has a crush."

I gave her puppy dog eyes.

"If you make me throw up in our cruiser, I will never forgive you."

A flush of heat crawled up my neck, and my lips parted wide.

"Fuck. You're grinning *and* blushing. This is bad. So fucking bad."

"Yeah, I think it might be."

Before she could say anything else, one of the guys in our unit rapped on the driver's-side window, nearly startling Donna into spilling her coffee.

"Sarge wants you two now. He's in a mood this morning."

We shared a look, and hopped out.

<hr>

We entered Brandt's office to find Detective Biel already sitting in one of the two chairs opposite the desk.

"Officers Frazier, Nuñez." Biel gave each of us a head bob without standing.

"Detective," we said in unison.

"Sit," Brandt ordered.

Donna complied; with no other chair available, I shut the door and leaned against the back wall.

"Judge Kenny gave us the search warrant this morning. Biel, how do you want to handle this?"

"I'll inform Mr. Shale, show him the warrant. Officer Nuñez and I will handle the search, along with a couple of the CSI guys. I'd like Officer Frazier to detain Mr. Shale."

Donna cocked a brow. "Why me? Can't another uniform babysit?"

"They could, but Shale knows you, and you've spoken with him a couple times. He might say something to you that he wouldn't to another cop. Eyes and ears open, okay?"

Brandt didn't give Donna a chance to reply.

"Good plan, Detective. Everybody out. I'm late for a meeting with the chief."

❖

We arrived at the Shale home a little after eleven o'clock. Donna and I stood behind Detective Biel as he knocked on the door. When it opened, Karl's eyes darted from Biel to Donna, then to me.

"Officers, did you catch someone?"

"Why would you ask that, Mr. Shale?" Biel asked.

"Because there's three of you out here, and more in the street. Something must've happened."

"Unfortunately, no. We haven't caught anyone yet. We're following up on all the leads though." Biel extended his hand for Karl to shake. "I'm Detective Biel. I've been assigned to lead the investigation."

"What happened to those two?" He looked back toward us.

"They're still part of the team. A detective is added to lead an investigation when certain crimes are involved. Once your wife was found, this was upgraded from a missing person to a murder investigation."

"Oh," Karl said.

"I have a warrant signed by a judge to search your home." Biel opened a folded piece of paper and showed it to Karl. "This is your copy. You're welcome to read it before we begin, if you like."

"Why do you need to search my place again? Didn't you already do that?"

"We're just being thorough. Now, would you mind waiting out here with Officer Frazier while our team conducts the search?" Biel motioned to several rocking chairs on the porch.

"Uh, sure, I guess. Can I get my shoes?"

"Of course." Biel turned toward me. "Officer Nuñez, would you go on inside while I get the team together?"

I nodded, stepped forward, then followed Karl as he padded to his office, slipped into flip-flops, then headed back out to the porch where Donna waited. She did not have a happy look on her face. I couldn't blame her. She was as good as anyone—probably better—and here she was, assigned to babysit. Biel wasn't known for looking down on female cops, but I couldn't help but wonder if that played a role in his thinking, even subconsciously. I got shit for being gay, but no one ever pushed me aside for it. I gave Donna a nod, hoping she knew I understood. She just pressed her lips into a line and turned to talk with Karl.

When Biel and the two CSI guys entered, I followed, but walked straight to the purse Donna had seen before. It was still on the table. I opened it as wide as the mouth would allow, then snapped photos of its contests.

"Still there?" Biel whispered, careful not to let Karl overhear—we were standing just inside from where he and Donna sat.

I nodded and showed him the photo of Emily's billfold and keys sitting atop other normal items carried in a woman's purse.

Biel motioned to one of the CSI guys to bag the whole thing.

Biel and I took the back of the house, the bedrooms and two bathrooms, while the CSI guys worked the office, den, dining room, and kitchen.

"Nothing at our end, Detective," one of the crime scene cops said as we reconnected in the foyer. "Everything looks normal. We ran the lights over everything and didn't come up with blood traces or anything suspicious. Kitchen has some stuff piled up, but you'd expect that from a distraught spouse."

Biel nodded. "Okay. We didn't find anything either. Let's take a look in the garage and out back, then call it."

I followed Biel and the CSI guys into the garage. The kitchen looked pretty clean to me, but the garage was spotless.

"Anything different from your last visit?" Biel asked.

He waited patiently by the door to the kitchen while I walked around and scanned the garage.

"Everything looks the same," I said. "Other than Karl's car being parked on this side."

Biel gave me a questioning glance.

"His car was parked there." I pointed to the empty space. "He said he'd been working on Emily's car before she went missing."

"Huh. People don't normally switch sides," Biel said.

"Really? I wasn't thinking much about it."

"Yeah. Same with a bed. You know, *your side* versus *my side*? That sort of thing. That translates into a lot of things."

I'd never been in a relationship where I slept with someone and had no idea what he meant. Although, when I thought about it, I did sleep on the left side by my alarm clock and couldn't remember a time when I used the opposite side. Interesting.

Biel turned to one of the crime scene guys. "Get Mr. Shale to move his car out of the garage, then take a close look at the floor."

The guy glanced back at Karl's car, then nodded, opened the garage door, and walked toward the porch.

"You really think this is something?" I asked.

He shrugged. "I don't know. It's more than what we have, but yeah, I think it's weird, and I learned a long time ago to pay attention when something makes my Spidey sense tingle."

I chuckled at a detective invoking the legendary investigator Spider-Man.

He grinned back. "Fuck you, Smiley."

My mouth dropped at him knowing my nickname, and his grin widened.

"I do my homework," was all he said as Karl entered with his keys.

"Just back it into the driveway, please."

Karl looked perplexed, but nodded. A moment later, he was back on the porch, the garage door was closed, and all four of us were kneeling over the space where the car had been.

"Well, damn," Biel said.

"That's not oil." I pointed at several spots.

"Nope," CSI number one said as he shone a light on the area. A dozen more splotches appeared where his light touched. "That's blood."

"Alright, let's mark it and get photos, then you guys go all science on it."

I couldn't help the laugh that escaped, and everyone turned. "Go all science on it? Really?"

Biel had been so professional to that point.

He grinned and shrugged again. "Lighten up, Smiley. This just got fun."

CHAPTER SIXTEEN

SAM—HAT TRICK (TUESDAY, JUNE 16, 2:47 P.M.)

I was bent over the front of an ailing Ford Mustang with my hands deep in her belly when my phone chimed. I didn't normally stop work for a text, but some sixth sense I'd never experienced told me it might be from a certain police officer. I hadn't spoken with him since our date, and my heart fluttered at the thought he might've reached out.

It chimed again.

"Fuck!" I banged my head on the Mustang's hood. Wiping my greasy hands on a rag, I bent over my phone. It needed to be touched to activate the Face ID, but I didn't want to get the screen messy. So, I did what anyone would do: I leaned over and punched it with my nose.

"Are you sending someone Eskimo kisses?" Ty called from the bay next to mine. "You really are a sick dude."

I ignored my asshole friend as he laughed his ass back under a Pontiac.

It took three Eskimos to get the screen to light up. Sure enough, there were two texts from Miguel. I couldn't get the grease off my fingers fast enough.

SMILEY COP: HEY YOU. GOT GREASE UNDER YOUR NAILS?

SMILEY COP: I CAN'T STOP THINKING ABOUT YOU.

I nearly peed myself right there. Holy shit. He was thinking about me. The twelve-year-old boy inside took complete control and I did a terrible white man happy dance right there in my shop. God, please tell me Ty was distracted.

Thinking as quickly as I could, I typed back.

ME: HEY. I'M COVERED IN GREASE. I BLAME YOU.

Smiley Cop: We haven't lived out that fantasy … yet …

Me: STOP! You're making me blush right here in the middle of my shop. What will all the guys think?

Smiley Cop: Oh, I know what they think. They're jealous of you and your hot cop.

Me: You're not my cop. Why do I have to keep saying that?

Smiley Cop: Wait? Someone else thinks I'm yours already?

Me: Fuck. Just ignore that. I never said it. Argh!

Smiley Cop: You're pretty darn adorable when you're flustered.

Me: You can see me? Did you guys put cameras in my shop when that car was here?

Smiley Cop: You'll never know;)

Me: Great. Now I'll be paranoid all day.

Smiley Cop: At least you'll be thinking about me. That's definitely worth a little paranoia.

Me: You sure are cocky.

Smiley Cop: You're gonna love my cock.

Me: Oh god. He went full teenager on me.

Smiley Cop: LOL teenage boys are horny all the time and stupid enough to go for what they want regardless of the consequences. So, yeah, I'm 100 percent teenager over you.

Me: Um ... I think that was the sweetest thing any guy has ever said to me. Sorta. Maybe.

Smiley Cop: You loved it, and you know it. Stop denying your giddy side.

Me: Giddy side? Is that a condition? Is there a cream or treatment of some kind?

Smiley Cop: Ha ha. Just say you'll have dinner with me Friday night. I've got all the cream you need.

Me: Sweet Jesus. He's a preteen. Don't you have a criminal to catch or something?

Smiley Cop: Not until you say yes to dinner at my place.

Me: Fine. Yes. I guess I might be okay with seeing you again.

Smiley Cop: You're blushing. You want me. You've got a crush on me. You're sooooo crushing.

ME: WHAT AM I GOING TO DO WITH YOU?

SMILEY COP: I HAVE HANDCUFFS AND A NIGHT STICK. A BIG ONE. IT'S THICK TOO.

ME: THE SHOP IS NOW CLOSED. PLEASE TEXT AGAIN DURING NORMAL BUSINESS HOURS ... AND PLEASE REMEMBER TO WEAR PANTS.

SMILEY COP: HA. SEE YOU FRIDAY.

"He has a big, thick night stick? Really?"

I jumped so fast my phone flew out of my hand and skidded across the shop. I was so caught up in our exchange that I hadn't heard Ty sneak up behind me to watch my screen.

"Shit, Ty."

He laughed. "You're so screwed. Your cop—"

"He's not my—"

"I know! He's not *your* cop, but you want him to be. Admit it. You have a thingy for his thingy. I mean, damn, you're *still* blushing."

"Am not," I said in my most mature voice as heat flared across my neck.

"Are too. Bet you are. You so are," he mocked in a high-pitched imitation of a five-year-old. We were definitely regressing. This was bad.

"So, are you going out again?" he asked.

I nodded. "Friday night."

"That seems far away. Why wait?"

"It's when he asked me. I don't know. Other people have lives and shit. Friday's good."

He held up two palms. "Easy, cowboy. Don't shoot."

"Sorry. Guess I am a little worked up."

He grinned. "You're exactly what you're supposed to be when you start falling. It's good to see, Sam. You deserve to be happy."

"Falling? I'm not—"

He walked away before I could finish.

The last time I let myself feel something for a guy, he vanished without so much as a word. I'd tried to tell myself that hadn't mattered, that we were just sex-buddies on different paths, that it didn't hurt. I'd tried to believe it hadn't meant anything because I had plenty on my plate with the shop and my friends, well, my friend.

The idea of Tyler being my only real friend sent my mind down a darker path. Why didn't I get out more? Meet more people? Make more friends? I was a good guy. Hell, I was a great guy. Why was I hiding? Was I hiding? Was I afraid to put myself out there?

Maybe the Joe thing really had meant something.

I only knew one thing for certain: I wasn't falling for Miguel.

There would be no falling. I refused.

No tripping, no stumbling, no tipping—and *definitely* no falling.

CHAPTER SEVENTEEN

MIGUEL—THE BRIGHT LIGHT (WEDNESDAY, JUNE 17, 9:01 A.M.)

"I think I'm falling for this guy, Donna." I could barely contain my enthusiasm. "I mean, he makes me smile—more than usual, don't give me that look."

"You're always smiling, hence the nickname, genius." She rolled her eyes.

We sat on two rickety chairs outside the interview room where Karl Shale awaited his first in-house conversation with Detective Biel. This was a pivotal moment in the investigation, the one on TV where everyone hopes the cop outsmarts the bad guy and gets an 'Okay, I did it' style confession. Those rarely happened, but a cop could dream.

"Fine. I smile a lot. I'm a happy guy. Sue me." I shifted my chair to face her like we were on some game show giving clues. "But Sam's different. This whole thing is different. I know we've only been on a couple dates or whatever, but he's … he makes me feel … I don't even know how to describe it."

"Shit. You've got it bad," she said, like a doctor announcing I had cancer.

"You could be happy for me, you know. Just a little."

"Happy? I'm the one who scoops up all the pieces after you dream your way into a mess that falls apart. Remember me? Cleaning lady?"

"Oh, come on. That was just once. It doesn't even count anymore."

She snorted.

"I want you to meet Sam." Her eyes widened, and her mouth opened, but nothing came out.

"I'm serious. I can feel it. This one—"

Detective Biel interrupted whatever sunshine vomit was about to spew from my mouth.

"Ready for this?" he asked.

We nodded.

"I want you two standing against the far wall, watching him. He's been in there about an hour. You know the drill. Your eyes and ears will be better than mine since I'm asking the questions. We'll regroup after."

"Got it," Donna said as Biel entered the tiny room.

Karl sat at a metal table that was bolted to the floor. He wasn't under arrest, so there were no cuffs or restraints. When we walked in, he raised his head from where he'd fallen asleep on his crossed arms. His eyes were bleary and almost bored-looking.

"Black with one sugar, right?" Biel said, handing him a cup of coffee.

Karl nodded. "Thanks."

"Mr. Shale, we are recording this conversation. Officers Nuñez and Frazier will observe."

"Alright. But I still don't understand why we couldn't just talk at my house."

"We have some pretty crazy procedures we have to follow. Don't think any more of it." Biel smiled innocently. "Now, would you mind stating your name for the recording?"

"Karl Wilfred Shale."

"For the record, it is June 17 at 9:21 a.m. Present are Officers Miguel Nuñez and Donna Frazier. Mr. Shale, please state your address."

"Twelve fourteen Loan Oak Road."

"In Nashville?"

"Yeah."

Biel paused a moment and flipped open his notebook. I could see the pages were blank. It was all part of the show.

"I know you've told us what happened the morning you last saw your wife, but please go over it one more time. Start from when you woke up that day, before she left the house."

Karl blew out a breath. Most interviewees showed frustration when asked to tell the same story for the hundredth time.

"I got up around eight, I think. Made coffee. Went to my office. I take a minute to get going in the morning, but that's the best time for me to write."

"Okay. So you were writing in your office from eight until when?"

"I guess I stopped around eleven, maybe a little after."

"And you were writing the whole time?"

"No. I usually do thirty-minute sprints."

Biel scribbled a note. "What are those?"

"Time blocks. Writing is like working out at the gym for your brain. That muscle gets tired too, and needs a break before it can lift again."

"Makes sense." Biel nodded. "What did you do in the non-sprint time?"

"Worked on marketing stuff. Social media posts, that sort of thing."

Biel made another note. "What social media sites are you on?"

"Twitter, Facebook, Insta, TikTok, all the top ones."

"And you posted that morning?"

"Yeah. I post every day. If you don't, the platforms stop showing your posts as much."

"Did you get up at all?"

Karl cocked his head. "When? That morning?"

"Yeah. In one of those intervals when you weren't writing. Did you get up? Get more coffee? Grab a bagel from the kitchen? Go to the bathroom? Anything like that?"

Karl thought a moment. "I don't think so. I try not to drink more than a cup of coffee ... well, a mug. I make two cups and put them in a big mug. It keeps me in my chair."

"When did Emily get up?"

Karl's face fell as he thought. "I guess ... it was a little before I did, so seven thirty, maybe?"

"Did she have a normal routine in the morning?"

Karl shrugged. "Sure. She always got coffee and grabbed something to eat in the car on her way to work."

"Why didn't she go to work that day? It was a Monday, right?"

Karl nodded. "They'd had a big fundraiser that weekend. Lasted all day and night Saturday. I don't even remember her coming home Saturday night, must've been after I went to bed. She usually took the Monday off after events like that."

"Okay, so she'd taken that Monday off?"

"Yes."

"I'm sorry. I think I missed something. Go back to Saturday night. Did she not come home that night?"

"I'm sure she did. It was just late. She was always really late on the night of events."

Biel held his eyes a moment, then moved on.

"Alright. Keep going with Monday. You were doing sprints ..."

"Yeah. I think it was around eleven, might've been a little before, Em called out from the front of the house that she was going to the store. I wasn't really paying attention."

"Did you hear the door open and close?"

Karl shook his head. "I don't remember that, but I do remember hearing the garage door open because I get a chime on my phone when that happens."

"Oh, you have an app for your garage door?"

Karl nodded.

"I'll just need you to speak for the recording, please, Mr. Shale."

"Sorry. Yes, I have an app."

"Is there a camera?"

"Not on the garage, no. Just a sensor for when it opens and closes."

Biel wrote something in his notebook. "That was the last time you saw Emily? Or spoke with her?"

Karl nodded again, then corrected himself. "Yes."

"Is there anything else about that morning you can remember? Anything stand out as odd or unusual?"

Karl's eyes drifted left. "No. Don't think so. It was just a Monday."

"Do you know anyone who might've wanted to harm your wife? Anyone with a grudge?"

Karl shook his head firmly. "No way. She was the best. All she ever did was help other people and give back. Who'd want to hurt her for that?"

"What about in the charity? Did she beat anyone out of a job? Anything like that?"

He thought a moment. "Not that I know of. She would've mentioned something if there was bad blood. All she ever talked about was how the people at the center were like family."

"What about the people they helped?"

"The clients? Why would someone you're giving food and clothes to want to hurt you? That's nuts."

"Some of the people asking for help may have mental health issues or other concerns. Did she ever mention any of her clients, express concern about anyone?"

"No, never. I can't remember ... not even once."

Biel sat back and watched Karl a moment, then closed his notebook and stood.

"Thank you, Mr. Shale. Would you mind waiting a moment? I have something I need to do, then we'll wrap up."

"That's fine."

Biel made it halfway to the door before he turned back, as though remembering something. "Mr. Shale, do you know any reason why we would've found blood on your garage floor?"

Karl blanched. "Uh, no. Blood? Really?"

Biel nodded and sat again. "And not just a drop or two. Splatters. They were under your car, on the side you told us Emily normally parked."

Karl sat back. "Shit. You don't think—"

"You tell me."

"Me? I ... I don't ... I mean, how would I know?"

Biel waited.

"Look, I worked on her car, a lot. Piece of shit was always broken down. I had to take the whole engine apart just a week or so before."

"Did you cut yourself?"

He held out his arms. "I'm always cutting myself. You ever break an engine down?"

"No, can't say that I have." Biel glanced down. "I don't see any cuts or scars. Where would you have cut yourself, Mr. Shale?"

Karl flipped his arms over, revealing several large gashes with fairly well-healed scabs. "There's a couple."

Biel looked at the cuts. "Did you get treated for these cuts? Go to a clinic or hospital?"

Karl actually laughed. "For a cut? No, that's stupid. I just washed them off."

Biel glanced back down at Karl's arms. "Mind if I take a couple pics of those cuts?"

"Sure," Karl said, holding his arms out.

Photos snapped, Biel sat back and twirled his pen, tapped it on the table, then stuck it in his mouth.

"So, here's what I can't figure out," he said, tossing the pen onto the table. "The blood we found was directly under the car. There wasn't a single drop anywhere else. Not on the floor around the parking space. Not on the cabinets. Not on any of your tools."

"That's not weird. I'm kind of a clean freak in my garage. I must've missed spots under the car."

Biel nodded like Karl's explanation made sense, then rose again.

"Alright, I think that's everything for today. Let me check on one thing and we'll let you get on with your day."

The three of us left Karl in the interview room.

"It's not enough, is it?" Donna asked when we were well away from the door.

"No confession. No weapon. No motive. All we have is opportunity and a little blood, and we don't even know for sure it's the victim's. The cuts on his arms actually look about the right age. I'll have the techs check out the photos, but doubt they'll offer any help." Biel shook his head. "We should have the workup back on that blood next week. The lab's been slow lately. Until then, we keep at it."

"Well, shit," I said.

Biel nodded. "Exactly my thought."

CHAPTER EIGHTEEN

SAM—TURNING TABLES (FRIDAY, JUNE 19, 6:15 P.M.)

It took forever for Friday to get here. I felt like a kid waiting for Santa, checking the calendar every day to see if, magically, that day was closer than it had been when I'd looked five minutes earlier.

Alas, the calendar never cooperated.

Until it did.

"Why are Fridays the longest days of the week?"

Ty grunted a laugh. "You're pathetic, you know that, right?"

"What?" I feigned ignorance.

"You're so whipped. You've been on, what, two dates with the guy, and you're practically picking out curtains already."

"Oh, come on. Nobody's talking curtains. Cutlery and bakeware, maybe, but no curtains."

He rolled his eyes, but the smile beneath them shattered any seriousness in his tone.

"What is it about this guy? You were never like this about He Who Shall Not Be Named."

I chuckled. "You can say his name. Really, I'm okay. I guess it's just different. I mean, with Joe, there was never any expectation other than sex. It's what we agreed up-front. It's all he had room for in his life, and, at the time, all I thought I wanted."

"For three years? That's a long-ass booty call."

"Yeah, guess it was." I caught myself tapping my pen against my desk like I'd seen Miguel do a few times and grinned inwardly. I wouldn't dare tell Ty about that. He'd be ruthless.

"Anyway, it's different with Miguel. We haven't talked about what we want or anything, but I can tell he wants something more than just a hookup."

"You can tell that? After two dates?"

"Ty, I could tell on our *first* date."

He crossed his arms. "Okay, Oracle of Omaha, how could you tell?"

"That's Oracle of Wyoming, thank you very much." I grinned. He snorted. "The way he looked at me ... I know it sounds nuts, but he doesn't look at me like he wants to rip off my clothes. I mean, he does ... want to ... he wants to ... he did ... fuck. I'm babbling."

Ty nodded, his grin wider than ever. "Yes, you are. And that's how I know *you* want more out of this. I still haven't heard why you think he does."

"He offered to not have sex."

"What?"

I nodded. "That first night. We were kissing, and things were getting heated. He stopped all of a sudden and asked if I wanted to keep going. He said he didn't want to blow it by going too fast, that he knew I wanted to move slow, especially coming off the Joe thing."

"And did you? Take it slow, I mean?"

"We didn't have sex. Well, unless you count him hand-cuffing and blowing me until I—"

"I get the picture—and yes, that counts. The jury is unanimous. Although, you didn't do the big nasty, and I know you wanted to."

"Hey—"

"Don't deny it. I know you, Sam Prescott. You have the hots for this guy, and you want to screw his brains out."

"Okay, maybe. Sure. Wouldn't you?"

"Duh. Of course. He's fucking hot." He leaned back in his chair and stared at me for a heartbeat. "The fact you haven't … huh. Maybe you're right."I quirked a brow.

"Maybe he is different."

"He is, Ty. I really think he is."

I could see him standing in my doorway, taking off those stupid shades, slowly revealing his deep brown eyes and the tiny, upward curved lines that made his smiles so sincere. Before I knew it, I was grinning from ear to ear.

"It's good to see you smiling for a change. You can be a real prick when you're mopey."

"I've never been mopey—or a prick."

"Okay, maybe that's true. You're never a prick—but you have been mopey." He shrugged. "You've been more like a Disney character than a mechanic these past couple of weeks."

"Careful, flowers might start flying out my ass."

He laughed. "Please don't sing. I've heard you before. It's not—""Hey! I could be onstage!"

"Dancing half-naked on a pole doesn't count as *being onstage*, Great One."

"Many men like my pole-dancing." I grinned.

"Sam, you're whiter than that paper on your desk. *No one* likes your dancing. Trust me. Not even your cop."

"He's not my—"

"Yeah, yeah. When you stop daydreaming about your date, I'll let you finish that sentence." He stood and turned toward the door. "Can you please stop distracting me? My boss is a real prick, and I have a lot of work to do."

He barely made it out the door before I wadded up an invoice and tossed it in his direction. He peeked through the glass of the door and flipped me the bird as it fell harmlessly to the floor.

⸺◦⸺

Sam lived in an apartment not too far from my house in East Nashville. I'd driven by it a million times on my way to and from the garage. As I pulled into the parking space beside his cruiser, a little thrill ran up my spine. I'd never be able to see a police car the same way again.

I grabbed the six-pack of Corona I'd bought at a gas station on the way over, and strode up to his door. It opened before I could knock, revealing Miguel in a white apron that read, "Careful, this chef knows how to use his spatula." His face brightened as our eyes met.

"Hey," I said.

He stepped forward, grabbed my head, and pulled me into a passionate kiss. I nearly dropped the beer.

"Come on in," he said while I was catching my breath. "Dinner should be ready in a few minutes. Hope you like coq au vin. I started this last night. It should be really tender by now."

Holy shit. He started cooking our dinner the day before our date? And what's a coke-oh-vahn?

"Smells insane," was all that came out as I followed him toward the kitchen. Onions, wine, and richly seasoned chicken slammed into my senses, making my stomach roar.

He laughed. "Good, you're hungry. I've never learned how to portion control."

I set the beer down on the counter that overlooked the den, then turned to explore while he finished cooking. His place was tidy, everything in perfect order. He clearly had a better sense of style or decorating than me. It all seemed to match and flow—or whatever it's supposed to do. It looked good, but in an understated, modest way.

My eyes were drawn to a large set of framed police badges on the wall behind the couch. Some of them looked really old.

"Like the shields?" he asked from the kitchen. When I glanced up, he nodded toward the frame.

"Yeah, pretty cool."

"A lot of cops collect them. My dad got me into it a few years back. He gave me my first one. It's top left."

I climbed onto the couch. The first one was a plain gold shield with the words US MARSHALL embossed across the metal. It didn't look like much, but I could tell it was really old.

"It dates back to the Civil War, probably around 1864."

"No shit," I muttered, leaning in for a closer look. "Wow. It's so ... plain. Most of these others have fancy writing and colorful seals."

"Yeah. They've come a long way. They didn't even put badge numbers on them back then, so we have no idea who wore it. Last I checked, that one's worth about a thousand bucks."

I roamed the den, peeking at pictures and art scattered on shelves and walls. There was very little on display that offered more insight into Miguel, other than a couple pictures of his brother and sister.

"Not big on standing in front of a camera?" I asked as I sat at the kitchen counter to watch him work.

"Nah. Nobody wants this mug on film."

I totally would raced through my mind as he turned and smiled at me.

Damn, he was handsome—but not in the model-perfect, unattainable way. His imperfections made him more attractive: the tiny cut on his lower lip, a ruddy area on his right temple where he'd probably struggled with acne as a kid. Those places cried out to be kissed. They were part of him, and he owned them without shame.

More than his looks was his openness. There was a joy to Miguel that poured out of him. His whole presence screamed authenticity. There was something magnetic about that, something that begged to be known and understood.

He was handsome in a way that compelled me to ask and know more.

"Did I say something wrong?" He startled me out of my thoughts.

Without a word, I rose, walked around the counter, and wrapped my arms around him from behind. When I nuzzled my nose into the crook of his neck, he craned backward and purred. It was the happiest, most content sound I think I'd ever heard. I kissed his neck and pulled him closer into my body.

"God, that feels nice," he whispered. "But I'm going to burn your meat if you keep distracting me."

I gave him another peck, then stepped back with my hands up. "Sorry, Officer."

He shook his head. "Go open a couple of those beers and sit at the table. Dinner's ready. I just need to dish it out."

"Beer with Coco Chanel?"

"Coq au vin, you unwashed brute."

I raised my arm and sniffed my pit. "I bathed. Smells like Irish Spring. Want a sniff?"

"Wow. You really are twelve, aren't you?" He swatted at me with a ladle. "And beer goes with *anything*. I have wine if you'd rather—"

"Nope. Beer's great."

We finally sat. The table was laden with dishes of meat swimming in sauce, with carrots, mushrooms, and onions.

As I went to cut the chicken, it fell apart.

When I took the first bite, my eyes watered.

"Sweet baby Jesus. You never said you could cook. This is ridiculous."

He grinned. "I wanted to go to culinary school, but baseball called, then the whole cop thing happened."

I took another bite and groaned. "I don't care. Nothing matters but this food. Are you still here?"

His laughter echoed off the walls of the tiny kitchenette.

"Eat all you want. There's enough for an army here."

Two plates and three beers later, I sat back and rubbed my belly.

"You're going to make me fat," I said.

He glanced up, finished chewing, then said, "That assumed two things. First: I cook rich French dishes every day. That would definitely not be true."

"So, you were trying to impress me?"

He grinned and nodded.

"It worked. Damn. Impress me anytime." I took a last pull of my beer. "And the second assumption? You said there were two."

"That I cook for you often enough for you to gain weight. That would involve us seeing each other far more often."

I knew he was teasing, playing out the game I'd started, but something in his voice—and in his eyes—was testing. He was asking a question. He wanted to know.

I hadn't meant to answer, certainly not quickly, but "I'd really like to see you more often" fell out of my mouth.

"I'd like that too," he said, without hesitation.

And just like that, the army of butterflies started banging against the inside of my chest again.

Miguel looked away first, then grabbed his plate and reached for mine, but I blocked his hand as I stood.

"The dishes can wait," I said. His eyes widened, and heat bloomed between us. I took the plate out of his other hand, set it back on the table, and tugged at his wrist. He rounded the table and pressed himself into me as our lips and tongues found each other again.

On our last date, I was nervous. His confidence and forwardness had thrown me off my game. Driving to his place, I swore that wouldn't happen again.

And it didn't.

I gripped his wrists and pulled them behind his back. He tried to wriggle free, but I held firm.

"Oh no. You're mine tonight."

This big tough cop whimpered in my ear. He freakin' whimpered. And my cock hardened at the sound.

I walked him into a slim wall beside the fridge and pressed him roughly against it, never releasing his wrists or letting our lips part. After a moment, I flipped him around so his chest was against the wall and started yanking his shirt upward. He tried to help, but I playfully slapped his hands.

"Oh no. You don't get to help."

"Yes, sir."

I chuckled. That wasn't the game I'd intended, but it sounded damn hot.

"About time," I said as I pulled his shirt over his head and tossed it to the ground. His skin shone in the kitchen light, rich and tan. I gripped his chest with my hands, then nibbled on his neck. He shivered. Slowly, I ran my tongue down his neck, along his spine, savoring every curve and bend. When my tongue went dry, I kissed his skin and rewet it, resuming the trek down his back.

My hands found the button of his jeans and popped it free. I trailed my fingers along the outline of his hardened cock, begging to be freed from the denim. As slowly as my racing pulse allowed, I unzipped his fly to find a bed of brown curls springing free.

He wasn't wearing underwear, and I loved it.

He had to wiggle his hips to help me get his jeans down, but it was worth the effort. His perfectly round base-ball-player ass shone in untanned contrast to the rest of his body. Before his jeans hit the floor, I had his cheeks in each hand and was teasing my tongue along his flesh.

"God, Sam," he said, arching his back to press his butt into me.

I didn't have to be asked twice. My hands pulled his cheeks parted, and my tongue dove into his depths.

"Ahhh!" he called.

My shadow must've chafed, but I didn't stop, just speared my tongue deeper, swirling it about, tasting every bit of him I could reach. His hands flew down and gripped mine, squeezing tightly. I could feel his body tensing.

I'd wondered before if he'd enjoy feeling me inside him. I didn't wonder anymore.

"Get those jeans off and show me where your bedroom is," I ordered.

"Yes, sir," he said without turning around. His jeans were off in a flash, and he grabbed my hand and led me through the den into his bedroom. He leaned forward, as if to lay facedown, but I reached out and held him up.

"Not until I tell you, remember?" I gave his ass a light smack. He grunted, but I could tell he was smiling, even from behind.

"Sorry, sir. It won't happen again, sir."

"Better. You might be trainable after all." I glanced around. Bed, night stand, dresser, a fairly standard bedroom. "Where's—"

"Night stand drawer."

"Anticipating my needs. Good boy." I kissed his neck, then walked around the bed to open the drawer. A small bottle of lube and two condoms stared back. Either he was very active and was nearly out of supplies, or Miguel didn't get much action. Based on what I knew thus far, my bet was on the latter—and I intended to fix that little problem.

I resumed my place behind him and squirted a dot of lube on my hand, then teased the head of his penis. It jolted immediately.

"Sensitive, are we?"

"Uh, yes, sir. Yeah."

I grazed my slicked palm across his head, enjoying feeling him shiver again, then trailed wet fingers down the length of his shaft to his balls. With my hand against him, I could feel his pulse quicken. It was strong, powerful, and racing fast and hard.

When I pulled my hand away, he sucked in a breath.

"Easy. I'm not going anywhere." I pulled my own shirt off and tossed it where he could see it, then pressed my bare chest into his back. With one hand, I gripped his chest, with the other, his cock. With my mouth, I devoured his neck.

"Fuck, you feel so good, Sam."

"Tell me what you want. I want to hear it."

"I want to feel you."

"How?"

"Every way. On me, against me, inside me. Sam, I want you inside me."

I took my hand from his chest and pressed the still-slick finger against his hole.

"Yes! Please," he pleaded.

My finger moved past his entrance, feeling his fleshy warmth. He arched back again, and his hole tightened, gripping my finger. I slid it deeper, then almost completely out, then drove it in again.

"Fuck me, Sam. I need you to fuck me."

"Turn around." I pulled my finger free and stepped back. He turned.

"Take my pants off," I ordered.

He dropped to his knees, and his fingers flew to my fly. A moment later, I stepped out of my jeans and flicked them to where my shirt lay. Miguel's face leaned forward to take me in his mouth, but I put a hand on his forehead and stopped him.

"Oh no. You almost broke the rules again, boy."

He looked up, pure hunger in his eyes. "Sorry, sir."

"Turn back around and bend over with your hands on the bed."

While he complied, I ripped the condom wrapper, slid the rubber on, and slicked it with lube, adding extra to my palm. Once he was bent, I ran my hand over his hole, making him drip with oil. My dick was raging, so I pressed it into his crease. He craned again, begging for it. I tested his hole with the tip of my cock until neither of us could take it anymore. Gripping his hip, I slid myself inside him. Like a champ, he barely flinched. I could tell it hurt, but when I pulled back, he whimpered and reached back to pull me into him again.

"You want this?" I asked.

"God, yes.""Hard?"

"Please, sir."

So I slammed into him. There would be no more gentleness. He cried out, and I drove into him again. Over and over, until sweat covered both our bodies, and oil dripped onto the bed.

Without pulling out, I gripped his sides and helped him flip onto his back. I wanted to see him. I needed to look at him.

The moment our eyes met, my heart launched itself into my throat, and my mouth craned forward to meet his. His hands found the sides of my head as he pulled me into him. Our tongues tangled as our hands wrapped around each other. Primal thrusts had vanished, replaced by passion and lust. I pressed myself into him, slowly and deeply, feeling my full length fill him. Somehow, he filled me too.

Some moments later, when our bodies lay sweaty and spent, Miguel wormed his body closer so his head rested on my chest, just below my jaw. I felt his lips press into my skin, and I thrilled at the squeeze of his arm around me.

I hadn't planned to stay the night, but we fell asleep like that, slick and sated.

A noise woke me around two a.m. Sometime in the night, Miguel had shifted to the other side of the bed.

"Oh, god, another one. No!" he muttered in his sleep. I watched him push and turn, fighting against some enemy in his dreams. Sweat soaked the sheets. His voice, muffled by slumber, carried anguish and pain.

I scooted close and wrapped my arms around him. "Easy, Miguel. It's just a dream."

He jolted, then his hands found my chest and he shoved against me. "Stop! Please, stop—"

I leaned back, staring at him as awareness came into his eyes.

"I'm sorry. Sam, I'm so—"

"You're okay, Miguel. It was just a dream."

The look in his eyes as he woke told me it was far more than that.

"I'm sorry," he said. "I didn't mean to wake you. I hoped this wouldn't ... not tonight."

Unsure how to react, I gave him space, but asked, "Do you have these dreams a lot?"

He nodded without meeting my eyes.

"Work stuff?"

He nodded again.

"Do you want to talk about it?"

"No." He shook his head firmly. "God, no. You'd think I was cracking up or something."

"Miguel." I risked putting my hand on his shoulder. He didn't pull back. "I won't think anything. I'll just listen—if you want to talk. It's okay if you don't."

He finally looked up, and a long, uncomfortable moment passed. "Thanks, but I'm ... I'm okay now. I think it's passed."

"You sure?"

He nodded, then closed the distance between us and let me hold him until his breathing calmed and he fell asleep again.

My mind wouldn't let me drift off much that night.

CHAPTER NINETEEN

SAM – ALL-DAY AFFAIR (SATURDAY, JUNE 20, 8:25 A.M.)

The sun peeking through Miguel's bedroom window woke me around six fifteen. He still lay in my arms, sleeping peacefully. There hadn't been any more mutterings or nightmares.

I studied him, watched the rise and fall of his chest, traced the outline of his nose and cheek with my finger, careful not to wake him. I couldn't take my eyes off him. There could be no denying his handsome features: the square set of his jaw, his brilliantly white smile, the striking beauty of his toned and muscled body. But it was his inner strength that drew me in more than anything. I couldn't imagine the things this man saw on a daily basis, and yet he found a way to smile, to be a light for others when all else seemed dark.

My eyes rolled, as my subconscious mocked the silliness of my conscious thoughts. I'd been on three dates with this guy, and here I was philosophizing on his inner manhood.

That made me glance down to his outer manhood.

That was pretty too. Pretty and thick and long.

Just like that, morning wood turned into a rigid plank.

What was Miguel doing to me?

"What's that smirk for?"

Shit, he'd woken up.

"Uh, I was just ... um ... watching you sleep."

He nuzzled against me, and his eyes widened. "Apparently, you liked what you saw. Somebody's standing at attention."

My face flushed. He laughed and leaned over to kiss me.

"Oh, I have terrible—"

His mouth smothered mine, as his tongue delved past the morning fog toward my tonsils. It only took a second for me to stop resisting and throw myself into his touch.

In a heartbeat, our naked, unwashed bodies were grinding against each other, desperate for another round. Nobody called the other "sir." There was no wall-throwing or bending over tables. Our kisses were passionate and long. Our caresses were gentle. I didn't protest when he rested my ankles on his shoulders and reached for the other condom. I wanted him inside me, and he knew it.

Thirty minutes later, he held me in nearly the same position as I'd held him the night before. I couldn't remember ever feeling so at peace, so safe. When he kissed my neck as I'd done him, I pulled his arms tighter around me. We were tangled together, but I couldn't get him close enough. I needed more of him. I wanted more.

"I know we hadn't planned on waking up together, but I have an idea." His breath tickled my ear as he spoke. "Spend the day with me."

I hadn't seen that coming, and didn't know what to say.

"We can grab breakfast at the diner around the corner. I have tickets to the Sounds game this afternoon. I've been wanting to try that new Indian place out toward the airport. It's supposed to be great." He paused. "I mean ... if you want to. Don't feel—"

"Yes."

"What? Really?"

I could practically feel his smile through my back. "Yes, really. I'd love to spend the day with you. Will Annie be at the game?"

He chuckled. "Of course. She never misses."

"Good. I like her, and I want her to know I can be well behaved and not spill popcorn in her hair."

He squeezed me tight as he laughed. "That was so funny. You should've seen your face."

I tried to turn around, but he held me, then the fucker's fingers found my ribs and he started tickling my sides.

"You're gonna pay for this," I said through breathless laughter.

"Promises, promises."

⸻◆⸻

Breakfast turned into brunch thanks to yet another round of naked Twister.

Miguel was turning out to be a complete surprise, unlike anything I'd experienced before—and definitely unlike what I'd expected from the perpetually pleasant policeman.

Joe wanted to get straight to the point, to get naked and screw. There was no foreplay or teasing, unless I was in the mood to play master and draw things out. What we did felt good, but it was very one-dimensional.

It was so different with Miguel.

We'd only really been together a few times, but we already kissed and touched more than anything else. If I tried to jump ahead and, well, jump his head, he would press a palm to my chest and slow me down, kiss me tenderly, force us to take our time. With Joe, I knew it was just sex, that it was physical and meant nothing. I still wasn't sure what it meant, but Miguel's simplest touch felt more intimate than any sexual act I'd done with Joe.

I sat in the booth at the diner, staring out the window and daydreaming about the past week with Miguel. We'd finished our meal and paid the check, but Miguel needed to use the restroom before we left for the game. I wasn't paying attention when something tickled my hand.

"Hey," I said, smiling up. He sat beside me, grabbed my hand, and pulled me out of the booth. I caught a few glances from nearby tables, but Miguel was undeterred. He held tightly to my hand and led me out of the crowded diner toward our car. Holding hands might not seem like much, but that simple act, in the heart of conservative Nashville where the Bible has a belt, meant more to me than any date or sex or … almost anything.

As we climbed into my car, I turned and watched him settle in and buckle his seatbelt. He turned, cocked his head, and smiled.

"What's that look?"

My hand rose and cupped his cheek. Then I leaned over and pressed my lips to his. A heartbeat later—maybe ten, I lost track—I pulled back and, without a word, started the car and pulled out of the diner's parking lot. Miguel stared at me the whole time, that goofy grin sprawled across his gorgeous face.

⸺◦⸺

As we handed our tickets to be scanned at the gate, Miguel turned toward the concession stand to get the requisite pre-game beers. There was clearly a ritual to this experience, and I wasn't about to question it. Who turned away cold beer?

When we got to our seats, the entire row in front of us was empty.

"That's weird," he said.

"What?"

"Annie's always early." He pointed to her seat with his bottle.

We scanned the area, but Miguel's perky Broadway singer was nowhere to be found. Then I glanced out onto the field.

"Uh, Miguel," I said. "Found her."

His eyes followed to where I was pointing. There, in the grass between home plate and the pitcher's mound, was Annie, and a lone microphone on a stand.

"Ladies and gentlemen," the announcer called before Miguel could speak, "please stand and welcome Nashville's own Broadway star, Annie Riley, as she honors America with our national anthem."

"Oh my god. You're gonna get to hear her sing!" Miguel sounded like an excited little boy at his first game. He even craned his neck to get a better view and hopped a couple times. It was adorable.

With the first three notes, Annie gripped the crowd in her seasoned palm and held them throughout the final crescendo.

"She's amazing," I said, barely able to take my eyes off her as she waved to the crowd.

"She's seventy-seven years old. Look at her."

I looked around at the applauding masses. "They really love her. Wow."

"She does this a couple times a year, and a lot of the regulars know her. She's a super-fan. I didn't know today was one of her days."

"Will she come sit up here, or will they let her stay in the dugout or somewhere closer?"

"Oh no. She wouldn't dream of sitting anywhere but that seat right there." He pointed to her chair. "She's had that particular chair for as long as I've been coming here."

I looked around. There wasn't anything special about where we sat. We were midway up the stands on the first base side. There were plenty of better seats, and most of them were empty.

"Why that seat?" I asked.

Miguel shrugged. "No idea. I've never asked. It's just where she's always been."

Some local celebrity trotted to the mound and tossed the first pitch. It landed about five feet short of the catcher, but no one cared. The guy was famous and he liked baseball. That's all the fans needed to cheer him on.

Midway through the third inning, Annie appeared at the end of our row and began climbing over laps to her seat. Our entire section stood and applauded, sending a flush across her cheeks and a smile parting her lips. She lifted her chin and waved like the beautiful queen she was.

"Annie, your voice is amazing," I said as she pulled me down for a cheek kiss.

"Aw, thank you, dear." She waved a bony hand like she'd done nothing, but she swelled with pride.

The bats were hot, as both the Sounds and their opponents smacked home run after home run. By the bottom of the ninth, the score was tied at twelve. It took another five innings to decide the game, with the Sounds falling short by one silly mistake. With a runner on second, the center fielder bobbled a routine fly ball that would've ended the inning. Rather than throw to his cutoff at second base, he hurled the ball to home plate. The toss went wide and bounced off the brick backstop behind the catcher and ricocheted down the first base line, allowing the runner to practically walk home without a challenge.

The spirit of the Bad News Bears had visited the Sounds at the end of a fantastic performance. Unfortunately, the only thing the sports press would write about was the ending. No one cared how you got to the end, only that you won or lost.

"Well, that sucks."

Miguel and I broke out in surprised laughter at Annie's pronouncement.

"What? It did suck. Sucked a big one. That's what you kids say, isn't it?"

Miguel turned four shades of red.

I laughed so hard my sides hurt.

We each hugged Annie goodbye and made our way with the crowd to my car. The drive to the Indian restaurant took another forty minutes, thanks to post-game traffic, and there was a surprise waiting when we arrived. Thanks to COVID-19, the restaurant had converted to takeout only and had no plans to change back.

"Well, I guess we could go somewhere else," Miguel said. "I really wanted to try this place. Guys at the station talk about it all the time."

"Let's just take it home ... I mean, back to my place. My house isn't too far from here. We can pick up beer or whatever on the way there."

Miguel smiled. "Sounds good, but this is my treat."

"You don't have to—"

"I know, but I want to. I invited you. It's my date."

I grinned. "Your date. Yes, sir."

His eyes flared, and a smile that held more heat than warmth quirked his mouth. I had a pretty good idea what we'd be having for dessert.

"Stay here. I'll go order."

Before I could protest, he'd hopped out of the car and was entering the restaurant. Fifteen minutes and four radio songs later, the door opened and Miguel squeezed himself and three massive plastic bags into the front seat.

"Holy shit. Is there any food left in India?"

He chuckled. "Told you I've been wanting to try this place. I had to get a little of everything. Besides, they give cops a discount."

"Huh. Badge has its privileges, I guess."

"It comes with enough shit. It should offer some good stuff too."

That comment stuck in my head. It was the first time I'd heard him say anything that wasn't positive about his experience as an officer. A car filled with Indian food wasn't the place to ask about it, but I bookmarked the comment for a future conversation. It almost felt like he wanted to talk, but didn't even know how to start. Then I remembered his nightmare and wondered if there was some connection.

"Did I lose you?"

I startled and started my car. "Oh, sorry, just lost in thought."

⸻◆⸻

"That was insane. I think I gained fifty pounds." Miguel patted his completely flat belly as though it was rounder than Santa's. We sat on the floor of my den with our backs to the couch and legs stretched toward the TV.

I rolled my eyes.

"What was your favorite?"

"Shit. That's hard." He glanced down at the graveyard of empty takeout containers. "That shahi murg soup was incredible. I'd never had that before. But the eggplant thing ... what was that called?"

I grabbed the menu and scanned it. "Baingan bharta."

"Yeah, that." He laughed at my butchered pronunciation. "They made that really spicy. The only time I've had that before it was kind of bland."

I nodded. "That lit me up. Had to drink a whole beer so I could taste again."

He laughed. "You're such a wuss."

"Yeah, but you like me."

Something caught in his expression before he responded. When he did, his voice had lost its humor. "Yeah, I really do."

I awkwardly fumbled the menu. "I, uh, think the, um, lamb thing was mine."

"The lamb thing?" He chuckled. "Pronounce it for me."

"Amri ... tri ... no, shit ... amri-tsa-ri."

He gave me a round of mock applause. "Close enough. Personally, I like 'lamb thing,' maybe 'lamb thingy.' They should just rename it that. Definitely 'lamb thingy.'"

"Remind me why I like you, please." I smirked.

He sobered. "You like me?"

And suddenly, I was twelve again. "Yeah, I mean, of course I like … I mean, not *like* like … not … fuck. Yes, dammit, I like you. A lot."

"I … fuck, dammit, like you a lot too." He grinned, leaned over our empty plates, and kissed me.

"But—"

"Oh boy. Buts are never good. I mean, unless—"

"Shut it, you perv." I shook my head. "I'm serious. I need to ask you something."

He sat up straight and smoothed his face.

"You don't have to talk about it. I totally get it if you don't want to, but I have to ask."

"Shit, now you're scaring me."

"The other night, I heard you in your sleep. You sounded so … I don't know. Scared isn't right. Something. In pain? It hurt to hear you sound like that. You kept repeating the same phrase, over and over."

"What did I say?"

"'Not another one.'"

His eyes drifted to some point behind me, though I was sure he wasn't seeing anything in my apartment. I waited a couple minutes, but he still didn't speak.

"Miguel, you were shaking ... tossing and turning like you were struggling, or, I don't know, fighting something. I grabbed you and held you close until you stilled. I didn't know what else to do."

When another moment passed without him saying a word, I put my hand on his and asked, "Are you okay?"

He yanked his hand back like I'd burned him and held it to his chest.

"I'm fine. It was just a nightmare. I'm alright."

"Are you sure—"

"There's nothing to talk about. I'm good." He rose and began clearing our plates. I stayed on the floor, watching him. His movements were stiff and slow, as though he was wading through water or sand. When all the containers were trashed, and the plates rinsed, he returned to the den and sat on the corner of the couch farthest from me.

Still unsure, I pretended to flip through the menu.

His voice, when he spoke, was hoarse and low.

"My first was seven."

I turned to see a tear trailing down his cheek.

"She was only seven, Sam." He wiped the tear. "We'd gotten a domestic abuse call. Seems like we get a hundred of those a day. I didn't think much of it. It's usually noth-ing."

He rocked forward and hugged himself.

"This wasn't nothing. The bastard father—if you can even call him that—had ... he'd hit her ... Sam, he'd hit her with a hammer. She was seven."

Any semblance of control shattered, and Miguel began to sob. Tears rushed out of him as his shoulders and chest heaved. I tossed the menu and sat beside him. He fell into me before my arms could reach around him.

"God, Sam, she was so beautiful, and so small. She had long blonde hair. I can still see it, spread all over the floor around her head like a halo. It was so clear and golden ... until the blood soaked through from underneath. And that poor girl—"

I gripped him with all my strength as his grief shook us both. I didn't dare speak. What could I even say?

"Eva," he said through labored breaths. "That was her name. She loved angels and fairies. Posters covered her pink walls. And there were these tiny stuffed bears all over her room, must've been a hundred or more. Every color you could imagine. Some had little hats, like they were cops or firemen or whatever. I remember every one of them. They stared at me, Sam, the whole time ... the whole time I was there, with her. She couldn't, so they did."

His sobs grew, and my own tears flowed through his pain.

I don't remember how long I held him, how long we wept together, mourning a little girl I'd never met.

"That was six years ago." He finally pushed himself off my chest and rubbed his reddened eyes. "Donna and I had just been partnered, and we got that call. I'd seen dead bodies in car accidents before, but never anything like that. It's different when ... it's just so different."

He gripped my hand. It was drenched with his sorrow.

"Two weeks later, we got called to the scene of a homicide. Some woman had stabbed her husband a dozen times with a kitchen knife. That was a nasty scene, but nothing like Eva."

After another long moment, he met my eyes for the first time. "I try, Sam. I try so hard."

"You try what?" I asked.

"To see the good, to stay positive. That's what they teach us, that our work matters, that we make a difference. I try to focus on that and know I'm doing something important, but then I see Eva again ..."

"Just Eva?"

His lips pressed tight, and he shook his head. "No, not just her. David and Ella. William. Terrel. Candice. Ayisha and Tomas. Tomas was eleven." He wiped his face again. "I remember them all. Every single name. I want to forget, to be like those cops who treat each scene as something distant, but I can't. Sam, I'm right there. I'm with them. It's like they're begging me to help them, to make things right when there's no way—"

He put his face in his hands and I rubbed his back. Another ten minutes passed. I moved to the other end of the couch, pulling him with me.

"Just lay your head on my chest. You don't have to talk if you don't want to. Just let me hold you, okay?"

He settled against me, and I kissed the top of his head and stroked his hair. Within minutes, his breathing had slowed and I knew he'd drifted off to sleep.

CHAPTER TWENTY

MIGUEL—INNOCENT SMILES (MONDAY, JUNE 22, 9:17 A.M.)

I was late getting into the station Monday morning. I normally tried to get there around six to work out with a couple of the guys, then shower and change before roll call. For whatever reason, my alarm clock and I got into it pretty bad that day.

I'd left Sam's place around nine Saturday night. He asked me to stay over, but I needed some time to think. That's what I told myself anyway. The day had been a good one until I'd lost it on his couch. I still don't know where all that came from.

Sam held me for hours. It was the most peaceful sleep I could remember in weeks. Something deep inside told me that kind of rest wouldn't happen again soon, and I didn't want him to ... I couldn't face those dreams again with him nearby. I made up a lame excuse and came home.

Sunday morning was sunny and unseasonably cool for June in Nashville, hovering around seventy-five degrees. I made coffee, a giant bowl of cereal, and planted myself on the couch. Three baseball games later, the sun was fading, and I'd successfully wasted the day without encountering a single person or memory.

That was an accomplishment, wasn't it?

I slid into my seat beside Donna just as our sergeant took the podium.

"Cutting it a little close this morning," she whispered, glancing at me sideways. "Long weekend with lover boy?"

I grinned and nudged her knee with my own, then turned dutifully toward the front of the room where our supervisor was shooting daggers in our direction.

"Glad you could join us, Smiley," his gruff voice barked over the quietening cops. A wave of laughter rippled through the room at his use of my nickname and the ensuing blush that flooded my face.

"Mm-hmm," slipped out in a sing-songy Donna barb. I could see her maniacal grin out the corner of my eye.

The morning brief was uneventful. We moved with the mass of uniforms that drifted back to the cubicle sea where our desks waited.

"Let's grab some coffee." Donna wasn't asking. I could tell she needed caffeine by the tone in her voice, and I definitely needed an IV full of the stuff.

"Okay, talk," she ordered when the cruiser's doors slammed shut. "Something's off with you. Did Sam step on your dick or something?"

I coughed a laugh. Donna cursed like any cop, but she was selective when doing it. She never failed to catch me drinking or in a weak moment. I think she reveled in my shock.

"Sam is great. No, he's amazing. We had a really good weekend."

She cocked a brow. "Okay. Tell me about it."

"Really, I mean it. He's ... I really like him. I cooked for him Friday night, then we did brunch and a game Saturday."

"He slept over?"

"Yeah, well, we didn't sleep much."

"No details. Don't need details."

I chuckled. "Annie sang the national anthem at the game. That was cool. Afterward, we got Indian at that new place out by the airport. You know, the one I've been wanting to try."

"Yeah, the one you mention every time we're within ten miles of the place?"

"Right. Anyway. It was great. You definitely should try it sometime. Just tell them not to make it too spicy. I know you and your temperamental stomach."

"Duly noted. So, after Indian?"

I didn't mean to, but my eyes fell to my lap and I mumbled, "We just hung out, I guess."

There was a pause, then she said, "You guess? Hung out doesn't sound like wild monkey sex."

"Wild monkey sex? Is that even a thing? You straights do some weird shit." She crossed her arms, undeterred. "Everything was fine. He just held me on the couch, and I fell asleep."

"But?"

"No buts."

She laughed. "Oh, I'm sure there were *butts* involved. Don't make me count the ways."

I rolled my eyes and laughed with her. "Do you want me to describe how he used—"

"Absolutely not." She shook her head.

We pulled into the Dunkin' parking lot, but neither of us opened a door. She turned to face me, then put her hand on my knee. She *never* touched me. It was a professional line she wouldn't cross, despite us being close. "Sam, I can see something in your eyes. You're all smiles and everything, but I know you. What's going on?"

I thought about making up a story, lying and telling her Sam had a family issue or something, but I'd always been truthful with Donna. The last thing I wanted was for my demons to make me a liar too.

"I've been having dreams."

"Dreams?"

"More like nightmares, I guess."

She leaned back against the door. "Go on."

"Do you remember Eva?"

Her eyes widened. She nodded, ever so slowly.

"I see her, Donna, staring up at me. She wasn't even faceup when we ..."

A heavy silence was broken by some teenagers pulling up beside us and getting out of a Jeep. We watched them joke about as they made their way across the parking lot into the restaurant. They were so carefree, so young and unburdened. Watching them made the gloom welling inside me darken further. I was suddenly envious of their unseared eyes. My own burned at the thought.

"I see them all, over and over. Every night. Well, most nights. I try to shut them out, to squeeze my eyes tight and keep everything at bay. I try staying awake, watching TV, going for a run at crazy hours. Donna, I've tried . . . " My palms covered my face, and I fought back the waves threatening to spill over. "Nothing works. Nothing helps. I think those hours Sam held me gave me the first peaceful sleep I've had in ... I don't know. Forever."

"You told him about all this?"

I nodded. "I couldn't hold back anymore. It just came out. I didn't mean to. He could tell something was bothering me, and he kept asking. He was so sincere. I couldn't just ... I had to ... I—"

"Miguel, look at me."

My eyes gradually met hers.

"I see her too."

"What? You—"

She nodded. "Of course I do. How could I not?"

"I just thought—"

"That you were the only one? The only cop who struggled with the shit we see?"

I shrugged, and my gaze drifted back to my hands.

"I have this guy I see, a doc—"

"I'm not going to a shrink, Donna."

"It's not—"

"No. I can't do that. I won't."

She blew out a breath. "What about joining our group?"

I looked up. "Group? What group?"

"All cops. Cops who've been there, seen all of it. We get together, and, I don't know, just talk. Sometimes it helps to get it out. I know it helps to know there's somebody else who gets it."

"That sounds like PTSD shit, for vets and guys like that."

She nodded. "And girls ... *and cops*. We're vets, just of a different war. I'm no shrink, but PTSD seems to fit. We don't use labels or names. We just talk. And listen. It's helped me a lot."

"How long have you been going?"

"I started counseling a few months after Eva's case. Joined the group a couple years ago."

"You've been going that long? Struggling that long? Why didn't you tell me?"

"I didn't want you to think I couldn't handle it. You know? Like you couldn't count on me. It's hard enough being a woman on the force, but for guys to see you not coping—"

"I'd never ... shit, Donna. Please tell me I've never made you feel like that. I'm so sorry."

"Don't be ... and you haven't. Not even once. Just come to a group meeting with me. Even if you don't get anything out of it, it'll help me to know you're there."

When I didn't respond, a small voice asked, "Will you at least think about it?"

I stared out the window as the teens climbed back into their Jeep, all sipping from giant takeout cups. They were laughing and giving each other shit, being kids. Their smiles were bright and wide, like mine usually was.

I doubted there was darkness hiding behind theirs.

"Yeah. I'll think about it."

CHAPTER TWENTY-ONE

MIGUEL – THE CIRCLE (TUESDAY, JUNE 23, 7:15 P.M.)

I didn't want to go. No matter how much Donna said talking and listening helped, I couldn't get past the idea of reliving some of the worst memories of my life. How could that help anything? And how was me talking about those things meant to help other people? The only thing I'd be doing was planting those awful images into the minds of other cops. They had enough shit to deal with. They definitely didn't need mine.

Then Detective Biel dropped photos onto my desk.

I opened the file without thinking, and nearly lost it right there in the squad room, surrounded by cops, as

Emily Shale's lifeless image stared back at me. My shift had ended an hour ago, and Donna had already left for her meeting. My head shook as I dropped the file into my desk drawer and turned the key.

That's when I changed my mind. That's when I decided talking might not be such a bad thing. I didn't remember driving to the precinct where the meeting was held. I barely took note of the cops who greeted me as I entered.

There were five of us.

Donna leapt to her feet and raced to the door. There was pain and desperation in my eyes. She saw it. She wrapped me in a hug and held me right there in the doorway. I couldn't stop the tears.

A tall Black man with sharp eyes, also still wearing his uniform, sat opposite me in the circle of folding chairs. His name was Rick, and he wore the golden bars of a lieutenant. It struck me as odd to see one of the department's leaders at a group counseling session, though I should've known the brass saw just as much as we did—probably more.

Ken sat to my left. He was a beat cop, an officer who patrolled a neighborhood with the goal of really knowing its people and understanding the heartbeat of the place.

The trouble with getting close to a community came when members of that extended family suffered loss. Everyone felt it, especially those assigned to protect and preserve. It was etched across Ken's face.

Donna sat to my right. A woman in thick glasses with brown frames sat to her right.

"Everybody take a seat. Let's get started," the bespectacled woman said. Her voice was calm and pleasant; soothing. "Miguel, welcome."

I smiled weakly and nodded in return.

"There's usually a few more here. It's a small group tonight," Donna whispered. "I'm glad you're here."

I tried to smile.

I couldn't.

CHAPTER TWENTY-TWO

SAM: OPEN ARMS (TUESDAY, JUNE 23, 10:35 P.M.)

My phone rang a third time before I reached over to see who was calling so late. Miguel's face smiled back at me from the screen. He'd made fun of me for snapping that pic, but I wanted his face on my phone when he called. Color me cheesy.

"Hey, you," I answered.

"Hey."

I sat upright in bed. "Miguel, are you okay? It's half past ten. You sound—"

"I went to a meeting tonight. A session. I needed ... I don't know. It's just ... Sam, can I come over?"

"Of course you can. Where are you?"

"Well, um, in your driveway."

I laughed despite Miguel's somber mood. "Get in here, you big moron."

"Okay. Thanks."

I threw on some shorts and had the door open before he'd finished walking up the driveway. His eyes were hollow and red. His normally crisp uniform was crumpled. When he didn't make a snarky comment about me opening the door in nothing but shorts, my gut twisted. I grabbed him by his shoulders and pulled him into a tight embrace.

"Come in. You want something to drink? A beer?"

He shook his head. "Just some water?"

"One water, coming right up."

We settled onto the couch, Miguel pressed safely in the far end cradling his glass like it was a baby. I gave him his space and sat against the other arm, facing him with my legs folded underneath me. Neither of us spoke for a good five minutes. The room felt like someone had poured molasses everywhere. Our movements were slow. Even breathing felt labored. The pain on his face made my heart ache, but I knew better than to speak first.

"I went to this meeting tonight," he finally said while staring into his water glass. "Donna talked me into it. I guess she goes a lot, has for years. She'd never told me that."

He took a sip, then set his glass on the coffee table.

"There were four of us there, and some counselor lady. I just sat there and listened. I wasn't even sure why I went."

His voice was so small, and it lacked the joy and brightness I'd come to crave. It was like listening to a shell of Miguel, an empty, hollow husk of the man who brightened a room just by entering it. I wanted to cross the couch and wrap him in my arms. I wanted that so badly.

But I sat and watched and listened.

"They'd all seen some really bad stuff that stuck with them. One guy, a lieutenant, talked about having dreams like I do. A woman who'd been … a woman from one of his earliest cases visited his sleep. He said it happened almost thirty years ago, and she still comes to him every night. I just sat there. I couldn't believe it. Thirty years, Sam.

"Donna … God, Donna, she talked about some of the same shit I remember. Hell, we've been partners forever. We worked the same cases. She never told me she struggled with dreams or whatever. She's the strongest person I know. I mean, if she can't deal with this stuff, how—" He sucked in a breath.

"Then there was this woman. She'd been going to those meetings for years. Her husband left her, took their boys away. I guess she'd snapped a few times. She didn't really go into it too much, but you could see the guilt on her face. She'd done something that made her husband afraid, scared for their kids. She cried right there in the circle. It wasn't all quiet weeping, she screamed at the ceiling. I felt her pain every time she cried out her boys' names. We all gathered around and held her, one big hug. I didn't even know her, and my heart just—"

He finally looked up.

"How am I supposed to live like this?"

I started to move toward him, then caught myself. He saw the movement and scooted across to sit next to me. I took his hand in both of mine and stroked the back of it while he talked. Something inside him shattered in that moment. I could see it so clearly. Some wall that held him back—that shield of smiling perfection that kept every-thing held tightly—and it all just poured out.

Through tears and anguished breaths, Miguel told me about case after case. He relived finding victims in horrible states, some alive, others lost. He described personal items nearby, reminders of the life they once lived—the life they should've kept living.

A flood of tears flowed freely between us.

More than an hour later, he quietened. I still held his hand. He still struggled to meet my eyes.

Everything he'd told me was shocking, horrifying even, but none of it was unexpected. I knew cops dealt with terrible things. I guess I had never dwelled on it. It was their job, not mine. Everybody knew soldiers experienced PTSD. There were a million movies about it. But cops? They're supposed to be invincible, the guys and gals who stood between us and the bad guys. They weren't supposed to have trauma. That's what the T in PTSD stood for, wasn't it?

What Miguel said next shook me.

"You shouldn't have to deal with any of this, Sam."

My eyes widened.

"I know you don't want to. Who would? I should just go and let you live your life, let you be happy without all … without all this. You don't need my shit—or me."

It felt like he'd punched me in the gut.

I hadn't even thought beyond that night, about what it might mean if Miguel and I kept dating. I was so focused on his pain in that moment that I hadn't considered what it all might mean to me, to my life, to my dreams. We'd only been on a few dates. I hadn't thought much beyond the usual silly daydreams of a besotted boy.

Would it mean anything? Would it change anything for me? I knew the truth: it would change everything. How could it not?

I sat back, my mind suddenly spinning.

He clung to my hand, a drowning man grasping at floating wood.

Then something else struck me. As little thought as I'd given to the scenes that played in Miguel's mind, I'd given even less to those partners, spouses, and family members of cops who must also struggle as they watched their loved one wrestle with demons that couldn't be slain. They lived with the nightmares too. They might not see the scenes replayed over and over, but they dealt with the aftermath. They watched someone they loved struggle and hurt. Their relationships stretched and strained, sometimes frayed. They, too, were trapped in darkness with no way out.

How helpless they must feel. How hopeless at times.

In that moment, I glanced up at Miguel and felt that helplessness.

Sure, holding his hand offered comfort and safety, some support, but would it really do any good when he closed his eyes and—

But I wanted to do so much more.

I wanted to reach into his chest, grab those demons by the throat, and rip them free. I wanted to wipe his pain away and restore his beautiful smile. God, I wanted to save him, to heal him, to make him happy again.

I knew I couldn't.

Maybe nothing could.

But, looking into this man's eyes, I knew one thing: I had to try.

"Miguel, look at me," were the first words I'd spoken since we sat on the couch. His watery gaze slowly rose to meet mine. I cupped his cheek and wiped away his tears.

"I can't imagine what you've seen or what you're going through. I've never dealt with anything even remotely similar. I mean, I don't know how ... All I know is that I care about you—a lot—and I'm not going anywhere. Maybe I shouldn't have to face any of this. You're probably right.

But *you* shouldn't have to face it alone either. You hear me?"

"Sam, this isn't something you just slap a Band-Aid on. It could take years ... or I might never—"

I covered his mouth with a finger. "Stop. I get it. No quick fix. I don't know what's happening with you and me. Hell, I've never really dated. But I know one thing: I'm not planning on going anywhere. I like this guy I'm getting to know."

His eyes overflowed, but didn't leave mine. His cheek pressed into my palm, savoring the connection, and I felt his other hand leave mine and rise to press against my own cheek. We sat there on my couch, holding each other's cheeks without moving, staring into each other's eyes.

His voice broke as he said, "I don't deserve you."

I couldn't help myself. I smirked and said, "No, you really don't. But you've got me."

Through tears and pain, Miguel shook his head and laughed.

It was the most beautiful sound in the world.

CHAPTER TWENTY-THREE

MIGUEL – THE SECRET (THURSDAY, JUNE 25, 4:17 P.M.)

Detective Biel sat across the table from Karl. Donna and I leaned against the far wall. Karl glanced between the three of us, appearing bored. Everything in the room looked exactly the same as the first time we interviewed him, but nothing felt the same.

"Mr. Shale, since the last time we spoke—uh, last Wednesday—have you remembered or seen anything that might help us?"

Karl shook his head. "You're the ones supposed to be finding Emily's killer, not me."

Biel nodded. "That's true, and we're close, I think. Really close."

Something in Karl's defiant glare shifted, just a touch.

Biel opened his folder and ran his finger down the single-spaced text, as though searching for something. "Mr. Shale, who is Sandra Springer?"

There it was: a tiny hesitation, a catch in Karl's breath. Donna shifted beside me. She'd seen it too.

"I don't recognize that name."

"You don't know a Sandra Springer?"

"No."

Biel pulled out a photo and flipped it around so Karl could see it. "What about this woman? Do you recognize her?"

Karl studied the picture. No hitch. He shook his head. "No, should I?"

"That's Sandra Springer."

Karl's gaze darted back to the image. Too fast. There was something there. Emotion. Anger? His face smoothed almost as quickly.

Karl shrugged. "Still don't know her."

"Did Emily?"

"How should I know that?"

Biel pushed the photo toward Karl. He sat back as it edged closer.

"Do you know Emily's friends, her coworkers?"

"Yeah, I guess, the ones she talked about anyway."

"She never mentioned Sandra?"

Karl shook his head.

"Please answer out loud for the recording."

"No. She never mentioned any Sandra."

Biel sat back, then shuffled the pages in the file until he found the one he wanted.

"Let me read you something, see if it rings a bell."

"Okay."

"*Hey baby. I can still taste you. When can you come over again?*"

Karl glanced up at Donna, then to me, then back to Biel. "What? Am I supposed to recognize that? I don't even know who that's from."

"You know who it's to though, don't you?" Biel asked.

Karl started forward, then relaxed. "No. Who?"

"Let's try another one," Biel said. "This is in the middle of a conversation. *Your tongue felt so hot on my thigh. God, when you tickle my hair with your nose, it drives me crazy.*"

Karl held his features in check, but his face reddened slightly.

"That was from Sandra, Karl. Any idea who she sent it to?"

"How the hell should I know?"

"She sent it to your wife."

"That's bullshit—"

"No, it's not. We have Emily's phone, remember? It took our guys a few days to compile all the texts, but we have them now, all of them, and there are … well, a lot."

Karl no longer hid his anger. His forehead creased, and his mouth turned down like an ugly scar. The slight blush was now a bright, burning rage.

"The first one we found was from, let me see, 2019, over two years ago." Biel made a show of scanning pages. "Wait, that's not right. That's the first one we found that refers to sex. The first text from Sandra was from 2017. Let's see. In that one, she invited Emily for drinks. We think that was their first date."

"Date?" Karl's laugh was scornful. "That's not a date."

"What was it then?"

Karl seemed to gather himself and sat back, arms crossed. "I don't know. I didn't know any Sandra. I don't know what you're talking about."

Biel leaned forward. "Come on, Karl. You just said their first date wasn't a date. You practically spat it at me. I think you know exactly who Sandra is, and what she was to Emily."

"She was nothing to Emily. Nothing!" Karl shouted.

"Is that why you killed her?"

"What? No."

"You killed Emily, didn't you, Karl?"

"No. I didn't—"

"You were angry she was cheating on you, cheating with another woman. You were angry and hurt and disgusted—"

"Fucking right I was angry. Wouldn't you be?"

"What happened in your garage? That's where you killed her, isn't it? That's where we found her blood."

Karl's eyes widened. He clearly hadn't expected any of this.

"No, I didn't. I mean, I never hit her. I didn't kill her." He leaned forward and put his face in his hands. "I want a lawyer."

Biel stood and waited for Karl to say more. He didn't.

"Stay here with him. I'll be right back," he said to us before exiting. A few minutes later, he returned and nodded to us once, then stepped to Karl.

"Mr. Shale, you're free to go, but I would advise you not to leave the city. Do you understand?"

Karl glared at Biel, then strode out without a word.

"What the hell? I thought you were gonna cuff him," I said.

"No weapon, no confession, no arrest. Sarge wouldn't go for it. I tried." Biel gathered his papers and stuffed them in the file folder. "We'll watch him, see what he does. Today might spook him into doing something stupid. Beyond that, our hands are tied until we find something more solid."

"Well, shit."

CHAPTER TWENTY-FOUR

MIGUEL – SCARED LITTLE RABBIT (THURSDAY, JUNE 25, 6:15 P.M.)

Donna and I were packing it in after a long, frustrating day. From where we stood, Karl Shale practically admitted he'd known about his wife's affair, was pissed about it, and killed her for it. Okay, so he didn't admit to killing her, but he was trying to stab Detective Biel with his glares right before demanding a lawyer. That screamed guilt to me.

Maybe I just wanted resolution, to find the bad guy and see him in cuffs. That sight might not bring back a dead victim or ease someone's grief, but any cop worth their salt would admit it felt good seeing the guilty get what they deserved.

Karl Shale deserved to be caught and punished. I was sure of it.

"You up to anything tonight? Seeing lover boy?" Donna asked on our way out of the station.

"Nah. He works late on Thursdays, then hits the gym."

She raised a brow, and the corner of her mouth quirked upward.

"What?"

"You know his schedule already? Isn't that cute? My little sweetie-cop, all sappy for his grease monkey."

I tried not to blush, but the more her words sank in, the redder my cheeks turned. My grin practically hurt.

"It's good seeing you happy, Smiley. I'm just giving you shit."

Before I could think of a snappy reply, Brandt's voice bellowed across the parking lot: "Frazier, Nuñez. Squad car, now. Rabbit's running."

Detective Biel charged out of the station right as the radio on my shoulder crackled.

"One thirty-nine; ten eighty."

The dispatcher responded. ***"Go ahead, one thirty-nine."***

"One thirty-nine. This is ten eighty. Suspect driving white Ford Escort, Tennessee plate four-oh-seven-foxtrot-lima-five. Headed northbound on Gallatin Pike. Passing Cahal Avenue. Traffic is light. We're going fifty."

"Shit, let's go," I shouted as we ran for our cruiser. Donna flipped the lights, and we tore out of the lot.

"One thirty-nine, turning west onto Trinity Lane. Ran a red light."

"I-24 or Ellington Parkway?" I asked. Both were arteries headed north–south through the city and would afford Karl wider roads and more speed.

"Interstate. If he goes Ellington, we can get ahead of him."

We were still a few blocks to the west of the Cumberland River, on the edge of downtown. Even with our lights flashing and screamer going, it took too long to get to I-24.

"One thirty-nine. Turning north onto Ellington Parkway. Suspect cut off a blue Chevy. Ten fifty-one. Chevy is ten fifty-one."

Ten fifty-one meant the Chevy had crashed.

We finally hit I-24. It was the tail end of rush hour, and traffic was sluggish. Donna worked us over to the left lane and honked for people to clear a path. Some did, others struggled to move over. She hit the shoulder and pressed as fast as she could.

"One thirty-nine. Suspect getting onto Briley Parkway westbound. Repeat. Headed westbound on Briley Parkway."

Briley Parkway was the beltway that circled Nashville. This time of day, it would be crammed with commuters.

A high-speed chase would be dangerous. We reached the point where the interstate split, with 65 flowing right and 24 headed left. Donna floored it as 24 opened up. We were one exit away.

"One thirty-nine!" the cop shouted into his radio. **"One thirty-nine. He's pointing a gun at me. Dammit! He just fired. Shots fired! Shots fired! Two ten. Repeat. Two ten."**

"Fuck! I don't remember seeing a gun at Shale's place. Did you?"

"No." Donna's jaw clenched. She took the exit ramp for Briley Parkway and merged into traffic. We could hear sirens ahead of us. A few cars ahead, we could see everyone pulled over, giving us an unimpeded three-lane roadway.

"Hang on to your girdle," Donna said as she punched the gas. My stomach jumped into the back seat.

In seconds, two sets of blue lights came into view. I could see the white car leading them. Cars in front of the chase hadn't gotten the memo and were slowly moving out of the way. Shale's car bore more than a few streaks where he'd sideswiped those too slow to react.

We rounded the bend where Briley Parkway shifted from an east–west top of the circle into a north–south road. Shale was doing eighty on a stretch with a posted limit of forty-five, and it had rained late in the afternoon. He didn't make the turn, but neither did one of the cruisers.

"One thirty-nine! Ten fifty. Ten fifty."

We pulled to a stop as the officer of the crashed cruiser opened his door and reached his firearm between the window and windshield. An officer in the other car quickly followed suit. Donna wheeled around the side, and we both flew out of our doors and trained our weapons on the white car.

"Hands! Show us your hands!" one of the officers shouted. The driver's head turned and looked back. We couldn't see his hands—or his gun.

"HANDS, NOW! THROW THE GUN OUT THE WINDOW AND SHOW US YOUR HANDS!"

A second flew by. Then another. Then ten.

Finally, the window opened.

"SLOWLY!" the officer yelled. "TOSS OUT THE WEAPON."

The gun flew out and landed a few paces from the door, skidding across the pavement.

"Now, show us your hands. Easy."

One hand, fingers splayed, appeared out the window. Then a second hand appeared.

"Slow. Open it slow. Get your hands up."

The door started to open.

Donna muttered something into her radio, then whispered to me, "Three, two, one, GO!"

As the door opened fully, we raced forward. I grabbed his arm and hauled him out of the car, while Donna secured his gun. By the time the other officers got to us, Karl Shale's face was kissing the pavement, and his hands were safely cuffed.

CHAPTER TWENTY-FIVE

SAM – HOLY NEWSCAST, BATMAN! (THURSDAY, JUNE 25, 10:04 P.M.)

"Turn on Channel 4 right now," Tyler's excited voice barked through the phone.

"Hang on. I just went to bed."

"Old fucker. Hurry, before they move on to the next story."

I stumbled into the den and clicked on the television, which was thankfully already tuned to Channel 4.

"... won't reveal details, but sources hint at infidelity as a motive. No word on whether it was his or hers.

"Five bystanders were injured as the suspect fled author-ities. A police spokesman confirmed all officers were un-harmed, though one cruiser was involved in the accident that ultimately ended the chase. The suspect, thirty-five-year-old Karl Shale, husband of the late Emily Shale, who was re-ported missing on June fifth, led officers through the north-east heart of the city.

"Karl Shale is set to be arraigned on multiple charges tomorrow morning, and prosecutors say they plan to ask the court to hold him without bail. They would not confirm if murder was among those charges."

"Looks like they caught the guy. It was the husband, if you can believe it. He looked so sad in all the interviews." He paused a beat. "Your cop did it."

I grinned, pride swelling in my chest. "Yeah, looks like he did."

Ty laughed.

"What?"

"That's the first time you haven't fought me on him being *your*—"

Beep.

"Hey, that's Miguel. I'll call you back."

"Wait! I'm not done giving you—"

"Bye, asshole."

I mashed the button to pick up Miguel's call, making double-sure I didn't conference Ty in with us. That would be a disaster I'd never recover from.

"Good god, you're my savior."

"Oh boy. Do I want to know?"

"Nope. You really don't. Just ... next time you see Ty, would you tase him for me? Just a little?" I smiled as Miguel's rich laughter filled my ear. "So, I just saw the news. Wait, Miguel, shit. Are you okay? They said a cop wrecked his car. That wasn't you and Donna, was it?"

"Easy. I'm fine. Donna was driving, and she'd *never* let anything happen to her baby. Promise."

"Aw. You're her baby?"

He chuckled. "No. The cruiser. I'm just a passenger."

I took a breath and tried to steady my pulse.

"Thank god. I was—"

"Worried about me? Really?"

The cocky grin in his voice made my neck tingle. "Fucker."

"Careful what you ask for. I had a big day. I might need—"

"I liked you a lot better when you were all dark and brooding behind your shades. At least you were quiet then. Shut up and tell me about the chase already."

"How can I shut up *and* tell you—"

"Miguel!"

He chuckled again.

"We made an arrest," Miguel said. "The husband's in jail and will at least face charges on evading officers, shooting at us, and a list of others."

"No murder charges?"

He sighed. "We're still working on that."

"So the case isn't over? Really?"

He groaned. "Unfortunately not."

"I don't get it. You got your guy. Isn't running from the cops like an admission of guilt? It sure looks like that on TV. What's left?"

"Yeah, it looks like it, but it's not the same thing. Don't get me wrong, it helps. Juries don't trust runners, but that doesn't mean they'll convict him of murder." He paused, and I could tell he was deciding how much to tell me. "We're sure he did it. I mean, *I'm* sure. We have motive and opportunity, but we still don't have a weapon."

"You can't get a conviction without that, can you?" I asked.

"We can. It's just a lot harder. The DA will be all over us to find it now, not like we haven't been looking for weeks. But once there's an arrest, the clock starts ticking. There's only so much time to find the weapon before trial—or worse, before a judge decides we don't have enough evidence to even go to trial."

"You think that could happen?"

"Maybe. No, I don't think so. Who knows? The DA will know better. All I know is we stand a lot better chance if we find a weapon and whatever evidence is on it."

"Huh. Right. Makes sense." I really didn't know what to say. Outside of watching murder mysteries on TV, I didn't know anything about the criminal process.

"That's not why I called though. I mean, it is, but I also wanted to invite you to a party."

"Really? Okay."

"I meant to ask you about it the other night, but things got kinda … anyway. It's for Annie. Tomorrow's her birthday, and a bunch of us are throwing her a surprise party."

"All you had to say was Annie's name. I'm totally in."

"You're gonna love this. TPAC agreed to host it. Some of her old stage buddies are flying in too. I bet they all end up onstage." TPAC, the Tennessee Performing Arts Center, was the primary performance hall in the city.

"I never thought of myself as a Broadway gay, but this sounds like a blast."

He laughed.

"You're such a Broadway gay. All that grease under your nails? How could you not be?"

I had to cover the phone to keep my snorts from egging him on more.

"Pick you up around six?"

"Okay. Ty will give me shit, but I'll leave the shop a little early."

"You could bring him," Miguel said.

"What? Ty?"

"Yeah, if he'd like this sort of thing."

"He'd bitch and moan all the way there, but love every minute of it. I was just talking to him when you called. Let me call him back before he goes to sleep."

"Okay. See you tomorrow."

"Hey, Miguel?" I said.

"Yeah?"

"I really like hearing your voice before I go to sleep."

My heart stopped as the pause lingered.

"I miss you too."

CHAPTER TWENTY-SIX

SAM – BROADWAY BIRTHDAY (FRIDAY, JUNE 26, 7:00 P.M.)

Miguel's place was closer to TPAC, so I drove over and parked in his lot. I looked in the rearview mirror and fidgeted with my hair, despite it being buzzed down to nothing and incapable of moving or being out of place. I checked myself one last time, then hopped out of the car and made my way to his door.

Fuck, what's Miguel doing to me? I'm a nervous wreck—and I'm never nervous.

I smoothed a wrinkle out of my shirt and raised my knuckles to knock. The door opened before I hit the wood.

"Damn, son. You clean up." Miguel's eyes widened appreciatively, then roamed slowly down my frame. I'd never been to TPAC before, but everybody knew you had to dress up when you went to the theater. It was a thing, right? I wore dark slacks and a matching coat with a light blue dress shirt. I didn't own a tie, so we were screwed if that was called for.

Miguel, Mr. All-Over-His-Shit when it came to work, still wore nothing but a towel wrapped around his waist.

"Fuck me. You should go dressed just like that," I said, eyeing his clearly cold, perky nipples. He actually blushed. God, it was sexy.

"Come on in. I just need to throw on some clothes and toss goop in my hair."

"Goop?" I coughed a laugh as he turned to head into the bedroom.

"Yeah, it's the technical term. Don't hurt yourself with it."

I flopped onto the couch, resigned to the ten-minute wait required for Miguel to finish becoming presentable. The TV was on, and a newscaster was talking about the Shale case.

"Hey," I called out. "Anything on the case today?"

"Not yet. CSI guys went back to the house this morning. Another team searched where we found the car and body. They're probably still out there. Unless they found the weapon, I won't see a report before Monday or Tuesday."

"Shit. So still no weapon?"

"Doubt it. They would've called or texted."

I flipped absently through the channels, finally landing on *Family Feud*. It was mindless and made me laugh. I loved game shows.

Two questions later, Miguel appeared in the den wearing navy slacks and a pink dress shirt. The sleeves were crisply rolled, showing off the tan of his forearms.

"Oh, baby. Wow. You look great."

"Did you just call me baby?" He smirked.

"No. Absolutely not. It was just an expression. I did *not* use a pet name. You're not ready for that. You're far too sensitive."

He rolled his eyes. "Okay, lug wrench, let's go."

"Lug wrench? That's a terrible pet name."

"Not if you know how to use it."

I rose and headed for the car, shaking my head the whole time. As bad as his jokes were, Miguel made me smile more than anyone I knew. I had a feeling my cheeks were going to ache before this night was over.

<hr>

I'm not sure what I expected for Annie's birthday party. She was a sweet enough lady, and clearly a gifted singer, but I never expected to find the TPAC parking lot half-full. Men and women dressed in suits and sequins strode from the lot to the theater doors. A few more fabulous members of the flock wore colorful seventies pants that flared at the ankle. One even sported a mile-high neon pink wig.

"All this is for Annie?" I asked.

Miguel nodded. "You don't get how famous she is, do you?"

I shook my head. "I'm entertainment challenged. Couldn't pick a Kardashian out of a lineup, and definitely don't know anything about Broadway folks."

"You should definitely call them 'Broadway folks' when we get in there. They'll eat you up." He chuckled. "When she was in her twenties, Annie was one of *the* stars on Broadway. She even played a leading role in *Chicago* when it opened in 1975."

"Damn."

"You don't even know what *Chicago* is, do you?"

"I've heard of it, sure. It's a movie," I said sheepishly.

"I should probably hold your gay card for safe-keeping until this event is over. Someone will definitely try to revoke it if you say things like that." He grinned. "I bet there are a ton of old Broadway stars here. Annie wasn't just a huge talent, she was loved. She founded a couple charities that now work worldwide. She's something of a grandmother to all the young kids trying to make it in musical theater now. Everybody will be kissing and hugging. Brace yourself."

"Oh, okay, cool."

He gripped my shoulder. "You'll survive. I promise."

"My face give it away that much?"

"You're a bad liar, and I'm a cop. I know liars." He grinned, leaned over and gave me a kiss, then turned and climbed out of the car.

We joined the trickling stream of people headed into the theater. The moment Miguel opened the door, the sounds of hundreds of conversations layered on top of cheerful, fast-paced music slammed into me. The mood of the place was vibrant and carefree.

"Let's grab a drink and find Annie," Miguel said.

While we waited in line, several guys and a girl, all in their late teens or early twenties, queued behind us. They teased and laughed until one of them started singing. The others didn't miss a beat, joining in to form a chorus of perfect harmony.

"Wow. They sound like professionals," I whispered.

Miguel grinned. "They probably are. A lot of the people here will be."

"They're really good."

"Just wait. They have a few surprises planned for Annie that I think you'll love too."

Beers in hand, we strolled about, listening to various groups singing and chatting. I guessed there were a few hundred people in attendance—then we entered the theater.

"Sweet Jesus. How many people are coming to this thing?"

Miguel scanned the crowd. "They had around a thousand, maybe a little more, last year."

I whistled. "All for Annie?"

"For her—and her charities. Any money they raise goes to them. I'm sure you'll hear all about them throughout the night."

We made our way down the aisle to the foot of the stage where Annie stood surrounded. She smiled and laughed as the group chatted. Her very presence lit up the theater.

"She's really something."

Miguel nodded. Before he could respond, Annie saw us and waved us over. She wore a floor-length sleeveless gown made entirely of silver sequins that reflected light like a human disco ball. Her hair was pinned up, and a makeup artist had done a masterful number of her face. If I hadn't known the birthday we were celebrating, I would've thought she was in her forties, maybe late thirties. She was striking.

The moment we breached her circle, spindly arms wrapped around Miguel's neck and ruby lips planted themselves on his cheek, leaving a faint mark. My mind raced with ways I could tease Miguel about wearing lipstick when Annie released him and repeated her assault on me.

"Boys, I'm so glad you're here. Isn't this wonderful?"

"*You're* wonderful, Annie. My god, you look like you just stepped offstage." Miguel took her hand from me and twirled her about. The girly giggle that flowed out of her filled my chest with warmth.

"And you," he said, as she spun back toward the group, "look amazing in red lipstick. Should I be jealous?"

My hand flew to my cheek before I could think, and a chorus of laughter erupted around us. I glanced around to find the group grinning at me, and Annie beaming at her handiwork.

"Leave it," Miguel leaned in and whispered. "I'll get it off you later."

Damn if that didn't make my pants a little tighter and my blush deepen.

We stood and listened to the chatter around Annie for another few minutes. The lights in the theater flickered a few times, and Miguel nudged me.

"Time to sit," he said, guiding me by the elbow back to the aisle.

"Oh no, boys. Your seats are right where they always are: one row behind mine. Sorry there's no baseball tonight, only sounds." Annie giggled at her own double entendre, then gave her best game-show hostess arm wave aimed at two seats in the second row. Each bore a sheet of paper with Reserved for Miguel Nuñez printed on them.

Miguel put his hand over his heart and half-bowed toward her. "Thank you, Annie. This is great."

"Gotta take care of my boys," she said. "It's good to see you two together again. You make a wonderful couple. If I was little younger and had different plumbing ..." She winked, whirled around, and began directing the rest of her group toward their seats.

"Oh my god, she's hilarious," I said without thinking.

Miguel chuckled. "You have no idea."

We took our seats. Annie's head turned and bobbed as she chatted merrily with those around her, and everyone who passed by. She was a wonder to behold. After a few minutes of others filling the hall, the theater darkened. Sweeping music played over the speakers as an announcer's voice rang out.

"Welcome, ladies and gentlemen, to an evening of music and celebration. Please take your seats. The fun will begin momentarily."

I didn't recognize any of the performers who took the stage first, though a few of the songs sounded familiar. I think I'd heard one of them in a commercial or movie trailer. Each stood at a simple mic stand in front of a closed curtain. Miguel was glued to the stage, his smile wide and his eyes bright. Halfway through the second song, I realized he'd gripped my hand. By the end of that song, our fingers were interlaced.

I stared down, and my mind raced. I'd never held a guy's hand in public before. Hell, I'd never held a guy's hand before period. Prior to the sexcapades with Joe, I'd only ever been out with one man. We were young and horny. That summed up our *one* date, if you could call it a date. The sex was hot and sweaty, but I never heard from him again. I don't even remember if I got his last name or phone number.

And here I was, in the middle of a crowded theater, holding hands with a handsome, hunky cop. I watched him as he lost himself in the performance. My eyes traced the curve of his jaw, the lines of his smile, the lock of unruly hair above his ear that refused to lie down. I couldn't tear my eyes away from him.

His head turned, and he squeezed my hand. "Everything okay?"

"Yeah," I gulped. "I ... uh, yeah, everything's great."

His smile broadened. He scooted closer so our shoulders touched, his other hand reached across and gripped my forearm, and he gave my hand another squeeze. Then his head turned back toward the stage.

Several other artists appeared onstage, paid tribute to Annie, then sang something they thought she'd enjoy. Miguel had been right. The theater was filled with artists and musical lovers. Nearly a thousand voices joined in every song. It was like I was sitting in the middle of a swirling sea of music.

The performances appeared to be winding down when the stage darkened. A buzz rippled through the crowd. Annie sat forward in her seat, her hands covering her mouth. This was what everyone had been waiting for: the big surprise.

"Annie," the announcer's voice boomed. *"Someone special wanted to wish you a happy birthday. We tried to keep her offstage, but you know how persistent she can be."*

When the spotlight flicked on, revealing a woman in an emerald gown, a few people screamed in delight and the applause swelled. When she opened her mouth and sang her first notes, the place erupted. Everyone leapt to their feet, and even Annie was cheering loudly.

"Holy shit, that's Patti LuPone!" Miguel said. "Sam, that's Patti freakin' LuPone!"

Not wanting to dampen Miguel's spirit, I didn't ask who she was. I just nodded enthusiastically.

Annie was positively beaming, and I thought I saw a tear glisten in the stage light.

By the time Patti's first song was winding down, the crowd was already begging for more. She sang two more, then waited a solid two minutes for the crowd to settle and sit. The whole theater seemed to hold a breath as everyone waited for Patti to speak.

"Annie, my dear friend." Patti stepped to the edge of the stage and spoke directly to Annie. "My dear, *old* friend." Everyone laughed at the barb. "You look beautiful tonight. Simply stunning. Thank you for letting me be part of this evening. I'm so blessed to have been here, but even more blessed to have had you in my life these past thirty years."

A chorus of "aww" accompanied applause. Annie's shoulders began to shake.

"Annie, dear, you inspire me. You always have. Everyone knows how amazing you are onstage, but it's your life offstage that gives me hope for humanity. You truly are the best of us. Happy birthday, sweet lady. We love you."

A wave of emotion rocked the crowd. Annie was in a full-on ugly cry. Miguel had to wipe his face. I even got a little misty, though I wasn't entirely sure why.

Patti blew a kiss to Annie, then another to the crowd, and walked offstage to another thunderous round of applause.

We stayed another thirty minutes, laughing and listening to spontaneous songs that bloomed around us like a garden. Around ten o'clock, we made our way through the line to hug Annie and say our goodbyes. She practically vibrated with energy.

"That was really fun. Thanks for dragging me out here," I said as we headed to Miguel's car.

"You didn't get bored with all the singing?"

"Nah. It was great. They were all really good. And I, uh, really liked holding your hand."

He smiled, reached over, and held my hand until we reached the car.

As he started the engine, he turned toward me. "Stay at my place tonight? I'd really like to wake up next to you tomorrow."

"You bet. I'd love that."

CHAPTER TWENTY-SEVEN

SAM — PYRAMID (TUESDAY, JUNE 30, 8:15 P.M.)

I closed the shop around seven fifteen. There must've been something in the water around town because a flood of cars showed up needing oil changes and other routine services. We barely caught a breath from the time we opened. By the time I closed the bays and locked my office door, I was exhausted and starving. There was no chance of the gym getting a drop of my sweat after a day like that.

The list of restaurants that delivered to my house rattled through my head as I started my car, but my phone buzzed before I could settle on one.

"Hey, handsome. Beat anybody with your stick thing today?"

"It's a billy club, and I was saving it just for you."

"I'm just leaving the shop. I don't think Billy and all his clubs could do much for me tonight."

"Could they feed you?"

"Uh ... you're not being sexual?"

He laughed. "I'm always being sexual. But no, in that moment I was thinking about food. I'm a block away from that Indian place. I could grab us dinner and be at your place in thirty, maybe forty minutes."

"That sounds amazing. I really didn't want to think, much less cook."

"See you in a few."

I grinned down at my phone as Miguel's image faded. It was so weird. We'd only known each other a few weeks, but it felt like a lot longer, almost like we'd known each other for years. Maybe I was just tired and being dramatic. Ty would definitely say that was the case. Then again, he really liked Miguel, at least what he knew of him from my endless droning, as he'd come to refer to it.

I had just enough time to drive home, take a quick shower, and pop open a beer before Miguel arrived. Once again, he'd bought enough takeout for all the people in India. I had to walk out to his car to help with the bags.

"You said you were hungry," he said as I eyed the buffet that filled my kitchen counter. "And I've seen you eat."

"I'll never complain about food, but damn, this is a lot."

"Just get me a beer and I'll make you a plate."

"Yes, sir, Officer Bossy Pants."

He laughed and smacked my ass with a loud *pop*.

"Don't hurt your hand," I teased.

"That sounds like a challenge. Maybe I should—"

I shoved the lip of a beer bottle toward his mouth to stop whatever mischief was about to tumble out. He winked and took a long pull.

We ate on the couch while watching reruns of the eighties classic *The $25,000 Pyramid*, my all-time favorite game show. Miguel surprised me by playing along with the contestants once they got to the winners' circle.

"You're such a little game nerd," I teased.

He tossed a wadded napkin at me. "You're one to talk. Every time I come over you've got Game Show Network on."

"What can I say? I like to be mentally stimulated."

His grin turned lecherous. "I can think of stimulation—"

I groaned and held him back. "You know I always want your naked body and throbbing cock, you beast, but I really am wiped out tonight."

"Damn, a hard pass on monkey sex? Is that allowed?"

"You're impossible, you know that?"

He raised his empty beer. "Impossible to refuse? Impossible to ignore? Impossible not to love?"

I rolled my eyes. "Just impossible."

He leaned past my outstretched palms and planted a kiss on my cheek. "Want me to let you get some sleep? You do sound pooped."

"You don't have to go. I just don't have physical activity in me tonight. And don't make some remark about being in me."

He laughed. "I would never. I'm an innocent little boy."

I nearly spat my beer. "You're neither innocent nor little."

"Aww, such a sweet talker."

"See? Impossible. Just like I said."

Pyramid's familiar theme drew us back to the television, and Miguel grabbed my hand and settled next to me. Tiles flipped as the host read off comical category names.

"M ... M ... murder," drew confused chuckles from the contestants and crowd.

"I didn't even think to ask, how's the case?"

Miguel rubbed my arm as he spoke. "Same as yesterday. CSI came back with zilch. I'm not sure where we go from here. Detective Biel has us pouring over the file again in the morning to see if anything jumps out."

"Huh. It's not like on TV, is it?" He grunted. "Definitely not."

We watched the next couple rounds of clues and answers in silence, then I turned back toward Miguel.

"Something's been nagging the back of my mind, and it's just out of reach."

"About *Pyramid*?"

"No, dummy, about your case. You said your guys searched the house, the field where the car was found, and the area around where the woman lay."

He nodded, but didn't say anything.

"Were there any other places to search?"

"Sam, I really can't—"

"Okay, I get it. Just let me talk this out. It's gonna drive me crazy if I can't at least figure out what's tickling my brain."

"Alright, but I might not be able to confirm anything you come up with. You okay with that?"

"Yeah, of course." I thought a moment. "The car came to my garage early on, right? That was one of the first things found."

"Yeah."

"I don't know everything your guys did, but I assume they searched it pretty good?"

He smiled tightly. "They're the best. Dusted for prints, searched for DNA samples, you name it."

"They searched the trunk? Under the seats? Compartments? All that, right?"

"Yeah, even took some of the inside apart."

"What about under the hood?"

Miguel cocked his head. "Under the hood? I'm sure they looked under there. What are you getting at?"

"I don't remember your team taking the engine apart, or really looking at the engine all that much. I could see most of what they were doing through the bay wall's glass. There's a lot of heavy stuff in there, but that's probably a dumb thought. The guy would've had to take the motor apart to get to anything he could swing and hit someone with."

"Huh. I've never heard of anything like that. Sounds like something they'd come up with in one of those crime shows." He sat back and stared at me. "You're a lot smarter than you look."

"Hey!" I bounded across the couch on top of him and tried to reach his ribs. He was even more ticklish than I was, but he was also stronger. Before I knew it, I was on my back and fighting the urge to pee all over him—and the den.

"You don't look so tired anymore," he growled in my ear before raking his teeth across my neck. "Maybe we could take this into the bedroom after all."

"All that detective work got my blood flowing. I think I need help to get sleepy. Know anybody who could—"

His mouth smothering mine was the only answer I got.

We never saw what happened in the winners' circle.

CHAPTER TWENTY-EIGHT

MIGUEL – THE CRANKSHAFT (THURSDAY, AUGUST 1, 2:34 P.M.)

Donna and I had just walked into the station after a late lunch. She set her bucket-sized McDonald's iced tea on her desk and plopped into her chair.

"What's that?" she asked, pointing at a manila envelope on the corner of my desk. *Call me when you get back* was scrawled in large print on the front.

I picked it up and turned it over. "Huh, that was fast. I asked the shop guys to look at something. It's probably a goose chase."

She watched as I ripped the envelope open and pulled out three pages of a report.

"No. Fucking. Way!" I said, loud enough to turn the heads of the cops sitting nearby.

"What?" Donna was on her feet.

"They found what looks like DNA residue on the crankshaft."

"Woah. Slow down. What crankshaft? What are you talking about?"

"Sam and I were watching *Pyramid* the other night."

"Sam the mechanic with the giant lug wrench?"

A few snickers nearby told me we had an attentive audience.

I gave Donna an annoyed glare. "Yeah, that Sam."

She scowled and whispered, "Miguel, you didn't talk about the case with him, did you?"

"No, of course not. Everything he knows he saw on the news."

She relaxed a little, but still crossed her arms.

"Anyway. He saw a report about the case, and it got him thinking, replaying everything he saw when the car was in his shop. He said he never saw the team break down the engine."

"Miguel, why would they do that? There was nothing to make us think—"

"Just go with me here." I held up a palm. "He said something that got me thinking. He said there were a few parts in an engine that could be swung, something like that. You remember the marks on the victim's skull where a couple of the blows struck? Looked like little train tracks?"

She nodded, now fully alert.

"Well, after Sam planted that seed, I did a Google search of engine parts. Take a look at that." I handed her the printout showing the image of a crankshaft. "That's basically a metal bar with a big gear on the end. Look at the grooves on that gear."

"Shit, that looks like our head wounds."

"Yeah. And our guy said he worked on the wife's car a lot, had it taken apart. What if—"

"He used something like this and then put the car back together? Holy shit, Miguel. That's genius."

I shrugged. "Leave it to an author to come up with crazy shit."

Donna ran a hand through her hair, then looked up. "Wait, somebody drove the car across town, at least once. How hot does it get inside an engine?"

I handed her the report. "According to this, a hundred to two hundred thirty degrees."

"Crap. Even if you're right, there'd be nothing left." When I didn't say anything, she looked up and quirked a brow. "What? I know that smug look. Out with it."

I grinned. "According to the geeks, DNA starts to break down at three hundred seventy-four degrees."

Chapter Twenty-Nine

MIGUEL – FOUR OF A KIND (THURSDAY, AUGUST 5, 6:45 P.M.)

"Hurry up, it's almost on."

Miguel was like a kid watching the chimney for Santa's great arrival. He'd texted and called a dozen times throughout the day, insisting that I not turn the TV on or listen to the radio. Something had happened, and he was more excited than I'd ever seen him.

"Smiley, chill. I'm just getting us something to drink. Besides, Donna and Ty aren't here yet."

"I know! Dammit." He fumbled in his pocket for his phone and texted Donna. It was his fifth text to her since arriving an hour ago. His phone chirped a couple seconds later.

"What did she say?"

"I quote, 'Stop fucking texting. I'm almost there.' She's eloquent, as always."

I shook my head and laughed. "You want me to record this ... whatever this is?"

He smacked his forehead. "I'm so stupid. Yes. Record Channel 4 at seven. That's a great idea."

"Seven? The news?"

He held up a finger. "Don't even ask. I'm not telling. And yes, the news."

I shook my head again and punched buttons on the remote. Miguel threw himself into his spot on the couch and chewed his fingernails. He did that a lot. It's a wonder he had any nails left.

I handed him a beer and headed back into the kitchen to finish laying out plates for dinner. Miguel and I had been dating now for nearly two months. What started as an occasional date every four or five days had morphed into one of us sleeping at the other's place almost every night. Tyler teased us about turning into lesbians, renting a U-Haul, and getting matching Home Depot cards. I tried to fight him off, but he wasn't far from the truth. Watching Miguel from the kitchen, I couldn't help but smile. He made me happier than I'd been, well, ever.

There were still dark nights. His dreams came nearly every time he closed his eyes. I did the only thing I could think of: I held him while he battled his demons. I'd lost track of all the tears we'd shed as he would wake and tell me about his memories. The counselor in his group—he called it *his* group now—said it was good for him to talk about it. She was wary of me becoming his shoulder at first, but relented when Miguel told her I was the only person he trusted with some of his recollections.

He started seeing her individually a few weeks ago, in addition to the group sessions. They were doing a thing called EMDR, a therapy designed to help victims of trauma process and manage their experiences. In typical Miguel fashion, he described it as watching a little light while the therapist buzzed his hands. I did some research and learned that, while he'd described the physical me-chanics in reasonable lay terms, he hadn't touched on the mental aspect at all. Some researchers called the process a "reprogramming," not of the memories themselves but of how the person emotionally relates to those memories.

The whole science behind the brain fascinated me, and I vowed to spend a lot more time learning about it. Even if I couldn't be present in his sessions, I wanted to understand what he was going through.

Despite his short-term progress, he'd been right when he said it would be a long road ahead. There was really no end in sight. Even if he managed to overcome past horrors, his job forced him to face new ones far too often.

The therapist warned that things would get tougher before they got better. They'd be dredging up memories even his dreams hadn't revealed. She said they had to get through it all before he would start to heal. I hated the idea of watching Miguel in pain, but tried to focus on the outcome, the goal of him being able to live without nightmares haunting his thoughts.

I was proud of him for asking for help, for accepting it. The societal stigma of seeking mental health aid was bad enough, but in the police ecosystem, it was far worse. So many cops thought asking for help showed weakness in a world where the weak fell or died.

But they were wrong.

I knew it took incredible strength to reach out a hand and clasp another's.

When we'd first met, Miguel had said Donna would likely keep an arm's distance to anything resembling a personal relationship, but something had changed as they attended more group sessions together. I could hear it in their conversations, even with only hearing one side of them. They'd opened up to each other, and their partnership had deepened into a much stronger friendship. It still surprised me when he'd invited her to dinner tonight. Clearly, something big was happening.

I assumed it was related to Annie. The newspapers had printed a spread on her birthday bash and the surprise performance by a Broadway legend. Since then, she'd received a call from the folks in Tony land, indicating she was to receive some kind of major award at the next gathering of theater's elite. Miguel said it sounded like a lifetime achievement award, but Annie remained tight-lipped.

To celebrate whatever tonight's announcement was, I found Tony-shaped chocolates for everyone, and had music from *Chicago* queued up on my phone. Miguel would never let me live down having a showtune downloaded, but it seemed like the right thing to set the mood.

Someone knocked on the door, and Miguel practically hit the ceiling.

"Easy, tiger. It's just the door."

He flipped around to face the door, sitting up on the couch on his knees like some preteen boy. It was pretty darn cute.

"Hey, Donna, come on in." She made it two strides into my house before Miguel shoved me out of the way and wrapped her in a tight hug, lifting her feet off the ground.

"I've got a knife," she said, wriggling to free herself. "I'm going to stab you."

He swung her around so her feet dangled. "Go ahead. I'll arrest you. I hear you like handcuffs."

"Not as much as you two," she snarked as her feet hit the floor.

I tried to recover enough to say something, but Annie's melodic voice intervened.

"What's this about handcuffs and boys? I want to watch that movie. Is it playing here?"

We all burst out in laughter.

"God, this is going to be a long night, isn't it?" I said to Miguel.

"You have no idea, boss." Tyler must've arrived right as the women had. He sauntered into my house in jeans and a raggedy Led Zeppelin T-shirt.

"Everybody!" Miguel's police officer voice stilled the festivities. "Couch, now! It's seven o'clock."

"Jesus, can't a girl get a drink before she starts taking orders?"

Annie had Ty in stitches already, and it was clear the two would be inseparable by the end of the night. We were so screwed.

"Annie, I love you, but sit your perky butt down." He turned to me. "You, lug wrench, turn on the TV."

"Yes, sir, Lordly Officer Man, sir."

"Please, Sam, don't give him ideas I will regret in the station tomorrow." Donna patted my arm as she headed to the couch. There wasn't enough room for all of us, so Annie, Donna, and Miguel squeezed together, while Tyler and I sat in front of them on the floor. Miguel gripped my shoulders as the *Channel 4 News* theme song played.

"I think this actually started at six thirty. I recorded it," I said. "Miguel wouldn't let me watch it without all of you though."

"Shh. Here we go," Miguel said.

"An update to a news story we've been following for weeks now," anchor Marius Payton's baritone said through the speakers. *"A spokesman for the Nashville Police Department*

confirmed to Channel 4 News *that additional charges have been filed against thirty-five-year-old Karl Shale, of East Nashville, including first-degree murder for the slaying of his wife."*

"Shit! You got him, babe. That's amazing," I said, reaching up and gripping his hand on my shoulder.

"Listen." He squeezed.

"In a strange turn of events, police say the stalled case was finally cracked when mechanics within the department's motor services division disassembled the engine of the victim's car and found DNA on the crankshaft. Lab reports returned a positive match for the victim, thirty-one-year-old Emily Shale. Detectives also reported the pattern on the victim's wounds matched that of the gears on the shaft. Shale allegedly used the crankshaft to bludgeon his wife, then reassembled the engine to hide the evidence.

"Shale now faces life in prison without parole, if convicted. We'll keep you informed as this remarkable case progresses in court."

Co-anchor Tracy Kornet leaned across the desk. *"That must've taken some pretty amazing police work to find DNA on the inside of a car engine."*

"It's like something you'd read in a mystery novel. Really remarkable," Payton said.

The newscast moved on to other stories, but we never heard them. Everyone was cheering and chattering, then heading into the kitchen for much-needed drinks. I started to stand, but Miguel's hands held me down. Donna didn't follow the others either.

"Sam, I wish we could tell the world what you did here," she said.

I scooted around to face them. "What are you talking about? I didn't do anything but let you use my garage for a few days."

"Babe, you came up with the idea of looking in the engine. We might've never found that DNA without you. You helped solve this case."

Donna leaned forward and put a hand on my shoulder. "We can't bring victims back, but we can give them justice—and try to give their families some sense of peace. You helped us do that."

I was overwhelmed; I had no idea what to say. It felt like my whole body was stuck in my throat. I looked from Donna to Miguel, and each of them wore the same expression. My eyes fell, then slowly rose to meet Miguel's again.

"You got him, babe. I'm so proud of you."

He pulled me up off the ground and into a hug, then kissed me deeply. When I pulled back, Donna—the hard wall of a woman who never crossed the line—had tears in her eyes.

"Are you three gonna make out down there or come eat? Annie's hogging all the chicken." "I am not, you little shit! Don't make me—"

"The kitchen might need a police presence," I said. Donna and Miguel grunted and rose.

Annie hadn't been chosen for a lifetime achievement award. That news wouldn't come for another few weeks, but it did come. Our new little family gathered at my house for that occasion too. My gaze roamed around my crowded den at Donna, Annie, and Ty on the couch, then at Miguel in one of the cheap folding chairs we'd bought at Target so no one would have to sit on the floor. I'd never thought of my place as small, certainly not as *too* small, but it was suddenly bursting at the seams.

Miguel smiled up at me. He did that a lot. Smiley was the perfect nickname for him. Just the thought of it still made something tickle the back of my neck.

I didn't know what our future would bring, how we'd face whatever life would surely throw at us, but I had a pretty good idea this group would smile and laugh and cry—we'd do it all—together.

<hr>

Thank you for curling up with Sam, Miguel, and the rest of the gang. If you loved Wrenched, please take a moment to leave a review filled with stars. Your feedback fuels indie authors and helps other readers discover our work.

And don't forget your free gift! I'd love to send you a free copy of My Accidental First Date. Click Here to tell me where to send it.

Learn more about upcoming releases, works in progress, the crazy life of an indie author, and much more! You can find me on Amazon, Facebook, Instagram, Bookbub, Goodreads, TikTok, or my website at www.authorcasey morales.com.

Also By Casey

Raised by Wolves Series

Nashville Spicy Series

ABOUT YOUR AUTHOR

Casey Morales is an LGBT storyteller and the author of multiple bestselling MM romance novels. Born in the Southern United States, Casey is an avid tennis player, aspiring chef, dog lover, and ravenous consumer of gummy bears.

www.ingramcontent.com/pod-product-compliance
Lightning Source LLC
Chambersburg PA
CBHW060910210726
48293CB00006B/2045